Praise for *Starlings*

"Jo Walton's short writings have for decades been among the things that make the Internet worthwhile. She makes science fiction illuminate life. This collection lives up to its title: iridescent, dark, gregarious, talkative and ever ready to fly up."
—Ken MacLeod, author of *Newton's Wake*

"Stephen King once wrote that 'a short story is like a kiss in the dark from a stranger'—that is, sudden, pleasant, mysterious, dangerous, and exciting—and the collected short fiction of Jo Walton is exemplary of the principle."
—Cory Doctorow, author of *Little Brother* and *Walkaway*

"Walton's diverse collection of stories and poems sparkles with originality and fun. The joy of this book will linger with me for a while."
—Beth Cato, author of *The Clockwork Dagger*

"Exquisitely written feats of imagination, each one leaving an impression long after it's done."
—Kelley Armstrong, author of *Rituals* and *Led Astray*

"*Starlings* is a showcase of Jo Walton's diverse talents—a collection too varied to be summed up in a few words. From fairytale fantasy to hard science fiction, from laugh-aloud play script to finely crafted poetry, with a writing experiment or two thrown in, *Starlings* should delight Walton's existing fans and garner many new ones."
—Juliet Marillier, author of *Daughter of the Forest*

"Jo Walton's delightful collection, *Starlings*, runs the gamut from homemade fairy tales to hard-boiled cloned-Jesus detectives (just wait for the shaggy dog); to a play with figures out of Irish myth, and a talking dragon; to a selection of her fantastic poems. It's the kind of collection you can glide through, often while laughing out loud."
—Gregory Frost, author of *Shadowbridge*

"One of the things I love about Walton's work is her range of human possibility, from laughter to horror, but above all a reveling in profligate beauty. This collection celebrates the best in the human spirit."
—Sherwood Smith, author of *Rebel* and *Revenant Eve*

"This collection of fiction and poetry from Hugo- and Nebula-winner Walton (*The Just City*) showcases her trademark focus on genre and philosophical questions . . . Fans of the [short] form will have plenty to appreciate."
—*Publishers Weekly*

"Reading this collection felt like watching a wizard at the cauldron having fun with new spells . . . I recommend this collection to anyone who enjoys fantasy, Jo Walton's previous works, or wants to try shorter works before committing to longer ones."
—*Infinite Text*

Praise for *Necessity*

"Brilliant, compelling, and, frankly, unputdownable."
—*NPR*

"As before, Walton has done a superb job of world building and character development, giving readers a novel that both stimulates and satisfies."
—*Booklist*, starred review

"There's more substance here than in many actual philosophy books."
—*Romantic Times*

Praise for *Among Others*

"A wonder and a joy."
—*New York Times*

"Never deigning to transcend the genre to which it is clearly a love letter, this outstanding (and entirely teen-appropriate) tale draws its strength from a solid foundation of sense-of-wonder and what-if."
—*Publishers Weekly*, starred review

"There are the books you want to give all your friends, and there are the books you wish you could go back and give your younger self. And then there's the rare book, like Jo Walton's *Among Others*, that's both."
—*io9.com*

Also by Jo Walton

Sulien series
The King's Peace (2000)
The King's Name (2001)
The Prize in the Game (2002)

Small Change series
Farthing (2006)
Ha'penny (2007)
Half a Crown (2008)
Escape to Other Worlds with Science Fiction (2009)

Just City/Thessaly series
The Just City (2015)
The Philosopher Kings (2015)
Necessity (2016)

Standalone Novels
Tooth and Claw (2003)
Lifelode (2009)
Among Others (2011)
My Real Children (2014)
Poor Relations (forthcoming)
Lent (forthcoming)

Collections
Muses and Lurkers (2009)
Sibyls & Spaceships (2009)
The Helix and the Hard Road (2013) with Joan Slonczewski

Chapbooks
Sleeper (2014)
A Burden Shared (2017)

Nonfiction
What Makes This Book So Great (2014)
An Informal History of the Hugos (2018)

STARLINGS
JO WALTON

JO
WALTON
STARLINGS

TACHYON
SAN FRANCISCO

Tachyon Publications LLC
1459 18th Street #139
San Francisco, CA 94107
415.285.5615
www.tachyonpublications.com
tachyon@tachyonpublications.com

Series Editor: Jacob Weisman
Project Editor: James DeMaiolo

ISBN 13: 978-1-61696-056-8

Printed in the United States by Worzalla

First Edition: 2018
9 8 7 6 5 4 3 2 1

CONTENTS

Poems

This is for Alter Reiss,
who has this whole short story thing figured out

STARLINGS

From stellar nurseries a pulse of light
From far away and long ago, the dawn
Reaches to us to teach how stars are born
Freshly fledged starlings as they first take flight.
Though we can never know or reach those bright
Beginning stars, we see them being torn
From nebulas and time, through skies forlorn,
A swirling flock that glimmer through our night.
We ask ourselves, ah, what strange birds are these?
Whose wings can beat a message from so far
As starlight through the branches of our trees.
Photons cross years to tell us "Here we are!"
Illuminating new realities,
A flock of starlings from a distant star.

INTRODUCTION

The traditional thing to say in the introduction to a short story collection is "Here are some stories, I hope you like them." I can't say that, for reasons I will now explain.

For the longest time I didn't know how to write short stories.

That didn't stop me trying. I liked reading them, and I knew that they were often where the cutting edge of SF was. I had also read advice that said it was easier to sell short work than novels, and so starting writers should concentrate on them. This advice so didn't work for me. I sold novels before I sold anything short, because novels came naturally and short fiction didn't. Even when I sold some, they mostly weren't short stories. For ages I felt a fraud, because my short stories were either extended jokes, poems with the line breaks taken out, experiments with form, or the first chapters of novels. Once you're fairly successfully selling novels, anthologists and editors ask you for short stories, and I always had to say embarrassedly that I almost never wrote any.

I had published nine novels before I figured out short stories. In fact, I had written my Hugo and Nebula award–winning novel *Among Others* before I knew how to write short stories. So that career advice for writers isn't necessarily the way it has to work. Funny, that.

When you're writing a novel, you have a lot of space for things to happen and for the characters to show themselves and to generate plot for you. You don't have to make it all up. There's room for it to unfold slowly.

In a poem, you're focused on words. It sounds ridiculous to say that the art of poetry is making words say what you want, because that's everything, isn't it, from conversation on out? But poetry is about words and images and technique. I've always written poetry. This is my first short story collection, but it's my fourth poetry collection. When I was trying to write short stories at the beginning of my career, I was also writing poetry. I'd send them both out, and while they were both being rejected, they were being rejected in different ways. The short stories got form rejections, or at best "send us your next thing" rejections. The poetry got rejections that said it was great but not the kind of thing people could publish. This was a huge advantage, because it let me see that my short stuff wasn't good enough yet, whereas my poetry would be if there was a market. There are markets now—there has been a speculative poetry renaissance this century, it's wonderful. If I were starting off now, I'd have no problem selling those poems. But recognizing that the short stories weren't good enough was very valuable. Being nearly good enough is a very difficult state for a writer. This is when people start believing in conspiracies and needing an in with publishers and sometimes give up and self-publish, even falling for scams.

What I need to write is what I call *mode*, which is hard to describe but nevertheless essential. It has to do with where I am standing with regard to the text and the reader, which affects everything else. Anything I want to write has its own mode, and if I have the mode—the voice, and that stance, then maybe I can write it. Without the mode, I have nothing. All the ideas in the world are worthless to me without it—and ideas are often the easy part. One thing with this is that I can sometimes borrow mode—I'll look at the mode something else is written in and think what fun it would be to use it myself.

I did eventually figure out short stories while trying to help my friend Alter Reiss fix a story called "If the Stars . . ." that he eventually sold to the *Magazine of Fantasy & Science Fiction*. I read the beginning, the first few paragraphs, which were great, and I said, "I think this wants to be a novel, and maybe that's why you're having this issue." He said no, it didn't, and when I read the whole thing I saw that he was absolutely right. He then found a way to fix the issue and sold the story, but I kept on thinking about it. The end of that story wasn't heavy enough to hold down a novel. It was a terrific ending for a five-thousand-word short story, but it would have been too slight for a novel. And that's the secret to short things, and what I needed to think about when thinking about the length something should be: the weight of the ending.

I've shared this revelation with a bunch of people since 2011, and some of them have said "Aha!" and some have said "Well duh" and most have said "Huh?" thus proving that as Kipling said "there are nine and sixty ways of constructing tribal lays, and every single one of them is right." Writers are different and write in different ways, and there is no off-the-peg writing advice that works for everyone.

Pleased with this insight, I went on to write, and sell, a couple of actual short stories. Er, that is, specifically, two. You'll find them toward the end of this book. I continue to think of myself as a novelist and a poet and not really a short fiction writer at all.

So here in one place for your reading convenience are two short stories that I wrote after I knew what I was doing, two I wrote before I knew what I was doing, some exercises, some extended jokes, some first chapters of books I didn't write, some poems with the line breaks taken out, a play, and some poems with the line breaks left in. I do hope you like them.

THREE TWILIGHT TALES

1

Once upon a time, a courting couple were walking down the lane at twilight, squabbling. "Useless, that's what you are," the girl said. "Why, I could make a man every bit as good as you out of two rhymes and a handful of moonshine."

"I'd like to see you try," said the man.

So the girl reached up to where the bright silver moon had just risen above the hills and she drew together a handful of moonshine. Then she twisted together two rhymes to run right through it and let it go. There stood a man, in a jacket as violet as the twilight, with buttons as silver as the moon. He didn't stand there long for them to marvel at him. Off he went down the lane ahead of them, walking and dancing and skipping as he went, off between the hedgerows, far ahead, until he came to the village.

It had been a mild afternoon, for spring, and the sun had been kind, so a number of people were sitting outside the old inn.

The door was open, and a stream of gold light and gentle noise was spilling out from inside. The man made of moonshine stopped and watched this awhile, and then an old widower man began to talk to him. He didn't notice that the moonshine man didn't reply, because he'd been lonely for talking since his wife died, and he thought the moonshine man's smiles and nods and attention made him quite the best conversationalist in the village. After a little while sitting on the wooden bench outside the inn, the old widower noticed the wistful glances the moonshine man kept casting at the doorway. "Won't you step inside with me?" he asked, politely. So in they went together, the man made of moonshine smiling widely now, because a moonshine man can never go under a roof until he's been invited.

Inside, there was much merriment and laughter. A fire was burning in the grate and the lamps were lit. People were sitting drinking ale, and the light was glinting off their pewter tankards. They were sitting on the hearthside, and on big benches set around the tables, and on wooden stools along the bar. The inn was full of villagers, out celebrating because it was a pretty day and the end of their work week. The man made of moonshine didn't stop to look around, he went straight over to the fireplace.

Over the fireplace was a mantelpiece, and that mantelpiece was full of the most extraordinary things. There was a horn reputed to have belonged to a unicorn, and an old sword from the old wars, and a dragon carved out of oak wood, and a candle in the shape of a skull, which people said had once belonged to a wizard, though what a wizard would have wanted with such a thing I can't tell you. There was a pot the landlord's daughter had made, and a silver cup the landlord's father had won for his brewing. There were eggs made of stone and a puzzle carved of wood that looked like an apple and came apart in pieces, a little pink slipper said to have belonged to a princess, and an iron-headed hammer the carpenter had set down there by mistake and had been looking for all week.

From in between a lucky horseshoe and a chipped blue mug, souvenir of a distant port, brought back by a sailor years ago, the moonshine man drew out an old fiddle. This violin had been made long ago in a great city by a master craftsman, but it had come down in the world until it belonged to a gypsy fiddler who had visited the inn every spring. At last he had grown old and died on his last visit. His violin had been kept carefully in case his kin ever claimed it, but nobody had ever asked for it, or his body either, which rested peacefully enough under the grass beside the river among the village dead.

As soon as the man made of moonshine had the violin in his hands he began to play. The violin may have remembered being played like that long ago, in its glory days, but none of the villagers had ever heard music like it, so heart-lifting you couldn't help but smile, and so toe-tapping you could hardly keep still. Some of the young people jumped up at once and began to dance, and plenty of the older ones joined them, and the rest clapped along in time. None of them thought anything strange about the man in the coat like a violet evening.

It happened that in the village, the lord of the manor's daughter had been going about with the blacksmith's apprentice. The lord of the manor had heard about it and tried to put a stop to it, and knowing his daughter only too well, he had spoken first to the young man. Then the young man had wondered aloud if he was good enough for the girl, and as soon as he doubted, she doubted too, and the end of the matter was that the match was broken off.

Plenty of people in the village were sorry to see it end, but sorriest was a sentimental old woman who had never married. In her youth, she had fallen in love with a sailor. He had promised to come back, but he never did. She didn't know if he'd been drowned, or if he'd met some prettier girl in some faraway land, and in the end the not knowing was sadder than the fact of never seeing him again. She kept busy, and while she was waiting, she had fallen into the habit of weaving a rose wreath for every bride in the village. She had the best roses for miles around in the garden in front of her cottage, and she had a way with weaving wreaths too, twining in daisies and forget-me-nots so that each one was different. They were much valued, and often dried and cherished by the couples afterward. People said they brought luck, and everyone agreed they were very pretty. Making them was her great delight. She'd been looking forward to making a wreath for such a love match as the lord of the manor's daughter and the blacksmith's apprentice; it tickled her sentimental soul.

The little man made of moonshine played the violin, and the lord of the manor's daughter felt her foot tap, and with her toe tapping, she couldn't help looking across the room at the blacksmith's apprentice, who was standing by the bar, a mug in his hand, looking back at her. When he saw her looking he couldn't help smiling, and once he smiled, she smiled, and before you knew it, they were dancing. The old woman who had never married smiled wistfully to see them, and the lonely widower who had invited the little man in looked at her smiling and wondered. He knew he would never forget his wife, but that didn't mean he could never take another. He saw that smile and remembered when he and the old woman were young. He had never taken much notice of her before, but now he thought that maybe they could be friends.

All this time nobody had been taking much notice of the moonshine man, though they noticed his music well enough. But now a girl came in through the back door, dressed all in grey. She had lived alone for five years, since her parents died of the fever. She was twenty-two years old and kept three white cows. Nobody took much notice of her, either. She made cheese from her cows, and people said yes, the girl who makes cheese, as if that was all there was to her. She was plain and lonely in her solitary life, but she couldn't see how to change it, for she didn't have the trick of making friends. She always saw too much, and said what she saw. She came in, bringing cheese to the inn for their ploughman's lunches, and she stopped at the bar, holding the cheese in her bag, looking across the room at the violinist. Her eyes met his, and as she saw him, he saw her. She began to walk across the room through the dancers, coming toward him.

Just as she had reached him and was opening her mouth to speak, the door slammed back and in walked the couple who had been quarrelling in the lane, their quarrel all made up and their arms around each other's waist. The moonshine man stopped playing as soon as he saw them, and his face, which had been so merry, became grave. The inn fell quiet, and those who had been dancing were still.

"Oh," said the girl, "here's the man I made out of two rhymes and a handful of moonshine! It was so irresponsible of me to let him go wandering off into the world! Who knows what might have come of it? But never mind, no harm done."

Before anyone could say a word, she reached toward him, whipped out the two rhymes, then rubbed her hands to dust off the moonshine, which vanished immediately in the firelight and lamplight of the bright inn parlour.

2

It was at just that time of twilight when the last of the rose has faded into the west, and the amethyst of the sky, which was so luminous, is beginning to ravel away into night and let the first stars rub through. The hares were running along the bank of the stream, and the great owl, the one they call the white shadow, swept silently by above them. In the latticework of branches at the edge of the forest, buds were beginning to show. It was the end of an early spring day, and the pedlar pulled his coat close around him as he walked over the low arch of the bridge where the road crossed the stream, swollen and rapid with the weight of melted snow.

He was glad to see the shapes of roof-gables ahead of him instead of more forest stretching out. He had spent two cold nights recently, wrapped in his blankets, and he looked forward to warmth and fire and human comfort. Best of all, he looked forward to plying his trade on the simple villagers, selling his wares and spinning his stories. When he saw the inn sign singing above one of the doors, he grinned to himself in pure delight. He pushed the door open and blinked a little as he stepped inside. There was firelight and lamplight and the sound of merry voices. One diamond-paned window stood ajar to let out the smoke of fire and pipes, but the room was warm with the warmth of good fellowship. The pedlar went up to the bar and ordered himself a tankard of ale. He took a long draft and wiped his mouth with the back of his hand.

"That's the best ale I've had since I was in the Golden City," he said.

"That's high praise if you like," the innkeeper said. "Hear this, friends, this stranger says my ale is the best he's tasted since the Golden City. Is that your home, traveller?"

The pedlar looked around to see that the most part of the customers of the busy inn were paying attention to him now, and not to each other. There were a pair of lovers in the corner who were staring into each other's eyes, and an old man with a dog who seemed to be in a world of his own, and a girl in grey who was waiting impatiently for the innkeeper's attention, but all the other eyes in the place were fixed on the pedlar.

"I don't have a home," he said, casually. "I'm a pedlar, and my calling gives me a home wherever I go. I roam the world, buying the best and most curious and useful things I can find, then selling them to those elsewhere who are not fortunate enough to travel and take their choice of the world's goods. I have been to the Golden City, and along the Silver Coast; I've been in the east where the dragons are; I've been north to the ice; I've come lately through the very heart of the Great Forest; and I'm heading south where I've never been, to the lands of Eversun."

At this, a little ripple of delight ran through the listening villagers, and that moment was worth more than wealth to the pedlar, worth more than the pleasure of selling for gold what he had bought for silver. His words were ever truths shot through with sparkling lies, but his joy in their effect was as real as hot crusty bread on a cold morning.

"Can we see what you have?" a woman asked shyly.

The pedlar feigned reluctance. "I wasn't intending to sell anything here," he said. "My wares are for the lands of Eversun; I want to arrive there with good things to sell them, to give me enough coin to buy their specialities. I'm not expecting much chance to replenish my stock between here and there." The woman's face fell. "But since you look so sad, my dear, and since the beer here is so good and the faces so friendly, I'll open my pack if mine host here will throw in a bed for the night."

The landlord didn't look half as friendly now, in fact he was frowning, but the clamour among the customers was so great that he nodded reluctantly. "You can sleep in the corner of the taproom, by the fire," he said, grudgingly.

At that a cheer went up from the crowd, and the pedlar took his pack off his back and began to unfold it on a table, rapidly cleared of tankards and goblets by their owners. The outside of the pack was faded by the sun to the hue of twilight, but the inside was a rich purple that made the people gasp.

Now, some of the pedlar's goods were those any pedlar would carry—ribbons, laces, yarn in different colours, packets of salt, nutmegs, packets of spices, scents in vials, combs, mirrors, and little knives. He had none of the heavier, clattering goods, no pans or pots or pails that would weigh him down or cause him to need a packhorse to carry the burden. These ordinary goods he displayed with a flourish. "This lace," he said, "you can see at a glance how fine it is. That is because it is woven by the veiled men of the Silver Coast, whose hands can do such delicate work because they never step out into the sun. See, there is a pattern of peonies, which are the delight of the coastal people, and here, a pattern of sea waves."

When those who wanted lace had bought lace, he held up in each hand sachets of salt and pepper. "This salt, too, comes from the Silver Coast, and is in such large clear crystals because of a secret the women of that coast learned from the mermaids of making it dry so. The pepper comes from the Golden City, where it grows on trees and is dried on the flat rooftops so that all the streets of the city have the spicy smell of drying peppercorns."

"Does it never rain?" asked an old woman, taking out her coin to pay twice what the pepper would have been worth, except that it would spice her food with such a savour of story.

"In the Golden City, it rains only once every seven years," the pedlar said solemnly. "It is a great occasion, a great festival. Everyone runs into the streets and dances through the puddles. The children love it, as you can imagine, and splash as hard as they can. There are special songs, and the great gongs are rung in the temples. The pepper trees burst into huge flowers of red and gold, and the priests make a dye out of them which colours these ribbons. It is an expensive dye, of course, because the flowers bloom so rarely. They say it makes the wearers lucky, and that the dye doesn't fade with washing, but I can't promise anything but what you can see for yourselves, which is how good a colour it makes." He lifted handfuls of red and yellow and orange ribbons in demonstration, which were hastily snapped up by the girls, who all crowded around.

The whole company was clustered around the pedlar now, even the lovers, but the landlord was not displeased. Every so often, when he grew hoarse, or claimed he did, the pedlar would put down his perfumes or lengths of yarn and say it was time for them all to drink together, and there would be a rush for the bar. The landlord had already sold more ale and wine than on an ordinary night, and if the pedlar was having his drinks bought for him, what of it? The landlord had bought some spices for his winter wines, and a silver sieve for straining his hops. He no longer grudged the pedlar his corner by the fire.

The pedlar went on now to his more unusual items. He showed them dragon scales, very highly polished on the inside, like mirrors, and rough on the outside. He asked a very high price for them. "These are highly prized in the cities of Eversun for their rarity, and the young ladies there believe, though I can't swear it is the truth, that looking at your face in such a mirror makes it grow more beautiful." Only a few of the village maidens could afford the price he asked, but they bought eagerly.

The grey girl had been standing among the others for some time, but she had bought nothing. The pedlar had noticed her particularly, because she had not paid attention to him at first, and when she had come to watch, he had smiled inwardly. As the display went on and she stood silent, smiling to herself aside from time to time, he grew aware of her again, and wanted to bring her to put her hand into her pocket and buy. He had thought the ribbons might tempt her, or then again the dragon scales, or the comb made from the ivory of heart trees, but though he had sold to almost everyone present, she had made no move.

Now he turned to her. "Here is something you will like," he said. "I do not mean to sell this here, but I thought it might interest you to look at it, for it is your colour." He handed her a little grey bird, small enough to fit into the palm of the hand, carved very realistically so you could feel each feather.

The grey girl turned it over in her hands and smiled, then handed it back. "I do not need a carven bird," she said.

"Why, no more does anyone else, but I see it fooled your eye, and even your hand. This bird, friends, is not carved. It comes from the Great North, from the lands of ice, and the bird flew too far into the cold and fell to the ground senseless. If you hold it to your lips and breathe, it will sing the song it sang in life, and they say in the north that sometimes such a bird will warm again and fly, but I have never seen it happen." He put the bird's tail to his lips and blew gently, and a trill rang out, for the bird was cleverly carved into a whistle. They were a commonplace of the Silver Coast, where every fishergirl had such a bird-whistle, but nobody in the village had ever seen one before.

The grey girl raised her eyebrows. "You say that was a living bird of the Great North that froze and turned to wood?"

"It has the feel of wood, but it is not wood," the pedlar insisted.

"Let me hold it a moment again," she asked. The pedlar handed it over. The grey girl held it out on the palm of her hand where everyone could see it. "No, it is wood," she said, very definitely. "But it's a pretty enough lie to make true." She folded her fingers over the bird and blew over it. Then she unfolded her fingers, and the bird was there, to all appearances the same as before.

The pedlar drew breath to speak, but before he could, the carved bird ruffled its feathers, trilled, took one step from the girl's hand onto her grey sleeve, then took wing, flew twice around over the heads of all the company, and disappeared through the open crack of the window.

3

As the leaves were turning bronze and gold and copper, the king came into the forest to hunt. One morning he set off to follow a white hart. They say such beasts are magical and cannot be caught, so the king was eager. Nevertheless, as often happens to such parties, they were led on through the trees with glimpses of the beast and wild rides in pursuit until the setting sun found them too far from their hunting lodge to return that night. This was no great hardship, for while the king was young and impetuous and had a curling black beard, he had many counsellors whose beards were long and white and combed smooth. Most of them had, to the king's secret relief, been left behind in the palace, but he had brought along one such counsellor, who was believed to be indispensable. This counsellor had thought to order the king's silken pavilions brought on the hunt, along with plenty of provisions. When the master of the hunt discovered this cheering news, he rode forward through the company, which had halted in a little glade, and brought it to the king, who laughed and complimented his counsellor.

"Thanks to you," he said, "the worst we have to fear is a cold night under canvas! What an adventure! How glad I am that I came out hunting, and how sorry I feel for those of the court who stayed behind in the Golden City with nothing to stir their blood." For the king was a young man, and he was bored by the weighty affairs of state.

The indispensable counsellor inclined his head modestly. "I was but taking thought for Your Majesty's comfort," he said.

Before he or the king could say more, the king's bard, who was looking off through the trees, caught sight of a gleam of light far off among them. "What's that?" he asked, pointing.

The company all turned to look, with much champing of bits but not many stamped hooves, for the horses were tired at the end of such a day. "It is a light, and that means there must be habitation," the king said, with a little less confidence than he might have said it in any other part of the kingdom. The Great Forest had a certain reputation for unchanciness.

"I don't know of any habitation in this direction," said the master of the hunt, squinting at the light.

"It will be some rude peasant dwelling, rat ridden and flea infested, far less comfortable than your own pavilions," the counsellor said, stroking his fine white beard. "Let us set them up here and pay no attention to it."

"Why, where's your spirit of adventure?" the bard asked the counsellor. The king smiled, for the bard's question was much after his own heart.

The king raised his voice. "We will ride on to discover what that gleam of light might be." In a lower tone, as the company prepared to ride off, he added to the counsellor, "Even if you are right, and no doubt you are, at the very least we will be able to borrow fire from them, which will make our camp less cold."

"Very wise, Your Majesty," the counsellor said.

They rode off through the twilight forest. They were a fine company, all dressed for hunting, not for court, but in silks and satins and velvets and rare furs, with enough gold and silver about them and their horses to show that they were no ordinary hunters. The ladies among them rode astride, like the men, and all of them, men and women, were beautiful, for the king was young and as yet unmarried and would have nobody about him who did not please his eye. Their horses were fine beasts, with arching necks and smooth coats, though too tired now to make the show they had made when they had ridden out that morning. The last rays of the sun had gilded them in the clearing, touching the golden circlet the king wore about his dark unruly locks; now they went forward into deepening night. The sky above them was violet, and a crescent moon shone silver like a sword blade. The first stars were beginning to pierce the sky when they splashed across a brook and saw a little village.

"What place is this?" the king asked the master of the hunt.

"I don't know, sire. Unless we have come sadly astray it isn't marked on my map," the master of the hunt said.

"We must have come astray then," the king said, laughing. "I don't think the worse of you for it, for we were following a hart through the forest, and though we didn't kill it, I can't think when I had a better day's sport. But look, man, this is a stone-built village with a mill and a blacksmith's forge, and an inn. This is a snug little manor. A road runs through it. Why, it must pay quite five pounds of gold in taxes."

The counsellor smiled to himself, for he had been the king's tutor when he was a prince, and was glad to see he remembered the detail of such matters.

The master of the hunt shook his head. "I am sure Your Majesty is right, but I can't find it on my map."

"Let us go on and investigate," the bard said.

It had been the red gleam of the forge they had seen from far off, but it was the lamplight spilling out of the windows of the inn that the bard waved toward.

"Such a place will not hold all of us," the king said. "Have the tents set up for us to sleep, but let us see if we can get a hot supper from this place, whatever it is."

"A hot supper and some country ale," the bard said.

"There are three white cows in the water meadow beside the stream," the master of the hunt pointed out. "The country cheese in these parts is said to be very good."

"If you knew what parts these were, no doubt my counsellor could tell us all about their cheeses," the king said.

They dismounted and left the horses to the care of those who were to set up the tents. The four of them strode into the village to investigate. The bard brought his little harp, the counsellor brought his purse, the master of the hunt brought a short sword on his belt, but the king brought nothing.

The inn was warm and friendly and seemed to contain the whole population of the village. Those who were not there came in as soon as the news came to them of the king's arrival. The counsellor negotiated with the innkeeper and soon arranged that food and drink could be provided for the whole company, and beds for the king and the ladies, if the ladies did not mind crowding in together. The master of the hunt pronounced the ale excellent, and the villagers began to beg the bard to play. The rest of the company, having set up the tents and rubbed down the horses, began to trickle into the inn, and the place became very full.

The king wandered around the inn, looking at everything. He examined the row of strange objects that sat on the mantelpiece, he peered out through the diamond-paned windows, he picked up the scuttle beside the fire and ran his hand along the wood of the chair backs, worn smooth by countless customers. The villagers felt a little shy of him, with his crown and his curling black beard, and did not dare to strike up conversation. For his own part he felt restless and was not sure why. He felt as if something was about to happen. Until the bard started to play, he thought he was waiting for music, and until he was served a plate of cold pork and hot cabbage he thought he was waiting for his dinner, but neither of these things satisfied him. Neither the villagers nor his own company delighted him. The villagers seemed simple, humble, rustic; their homespun clothes and country accents grated on him. In contrast, the gorgeous raiment and noble tones of his company, which were well enough in the palace or even his hunting lodge, seemed here overrefined to the point of decadence.

At length the door at the back opened and a girl came in, clad all in grey and carrying a basket. The master of the hunt had called for cheese, and she was the girl who kept the cows and made the cheese. She was plain almost to severity, with her hair drawn back from her face, but she was young and dignified, and when the king saw her he knew that she was what he had been waiting for, not just that night but for a long time. He had been picking at his dinner, but he stood when he saw her. There was a little circle of quiet around the corner where he sat, for his own people had seen that he did not want conversation. The girl glanced at him and nodded, as if to tell him to wait, and went with her basket to the innkeeper and began to negotiate a price for her cheese. The king sat down and waited meekly.

When she had disposed of her cheeses, the girl in grey picked her way through the room and sat down opposite the king. "I have been waiting for you all my life. I will marry you and make you my queen," he said. He had been thinking all the time she was at the bar what he would say when she came up to him, and getting the words right in his mind. For the first time he was glad he was king, that he was young and handsome, that he had so much to offer her.

"Oh, I know that story," she said. She took his ale tankard and breathed on it, and passed it back to him. He looked into it and saw the two of them tiny and distant, in the palace, quarrelling. "You'd pile me with jewels and I'd wither in that palace. You'd want me to be something I'm not. I'm no queen. I'm no beauty, no diplomat. I speak too bluntly. You'd grow tired of me and want a proper queen. I'd go into a decline and die after I had a daughter, and you'd marry again and give her a stepmother who'd persecute her."

"But I have loved you since I first saw you," the king insisted, although her words and the vision had shaken him. He took a deep draft of the ale to drive them away.

"Love? Well now. You feel what you feel, and I feel what I feel, but that doesn't mean you have to fit us into a story and wreck both our lives."

"Then you . . ." The king hesitated. "I know that story. You're the goddess Sovranty, whom the king meets disguised in a village, who spends one night with him and confirms his sacred kingship."

She laughed. "You still don't see me. I'm no goddess. I know that story though. We'd have our one night of passion, which would confirm you in your crown, and you'd go back to your palace, and nine months later I'd have a baby boy. Twenty years after that he'd come questing for the father he never had." She took up a twist of straw that was on the table and set it walking. The king saw the shape of a hero hidden among the people, then the straw touched his hand and fell back to the table in separate strands.

"Tell me who you are," the king said.

"I'm the girl who keeps the cows and makes the cheeses," she said. "I've lived in this village all my life, and in this village we don't have stories, not real stories, just things that come to us out of the twilight now and then. My parents died five years ago when the fever came, and since then I've lived alone. I'm plain, and plainspoken. I don't have many friends. I always see too much, and say what I see."

"And you wear grey, always," the king said, looking at her.

She met his eyes. "Yes, I do, I wear grey always, but how did you know?"

"When you're a king, it's hard to get away from being part

37

of a story," he said. "Those stories you mentioned aren't about us. They're about a king and a village girl and a next generation of stories. I'd like to make a new story that was about you and me, the people we really are, getting to know each other." He put out his hand to her.

"Oh, that's hard," she said, ignoring his hand. "That's very hard. Would I have to give up being a silver salmon leaping in the stream at twilight?"

"Not if that's who you are," he said, his green eyes steady on hers.

"Would I have to stop being a grey cat slipping through the dusky shadows, seeing what's to be seen?"

"Not if that's who you are," he said, unwavering.

"Would I have to stop being a grey girl who lives alone and makes the cheeses, who walks along the edges of stories but never steps into them?"

"Not if that's who you are," said the king. "But I'm asking you to step into a new story, a story that's never been before, to shape it with me."

"Oh, that's hard," she said, but she put her hand on the king's hand where it lay on the rough wooden table. "You've no sons, have you?"

"No sons, but I have two younger brothers," he said, exhilaration sweeping through him.

She looked around the room. "Your fine bard is singing a song, and your master of the hunt is eating cheese. Your counsellor is taking counsel with the innkeeper, and no doubt hearing all about the affairs of the village. Your lords and ladies are drinking and eating and patronising the villagers. If you really want to give up being a king and step into a new story with me, now is the time."

"What do I have to do?" he asked, very quietly, then she pulled his hand and for a moment he felt himself falling.

It was a little while before anyone noticed he had gone, and by then nobody remembered seeing the two cats slipping away between the tables, one grey and one a long-haired black with big green eyes.

JANE AUSTEN
TO CASSANDRA

D earest Cassandra,

We thought to have removed to Winchester by now, but Eliza has taken a chill and so we stay here another week, and you should not expect us to join you until after Whitsun.

Let me explain to you the advantages of remaining longer in this neighbourhood—there are two tolerable walks, one linen draper, with very poor stock, our apartments remain as unsuitable as I explained in my last letter, and Aunt Tilson has not learned the knack of keeping good servants. Nevertheless, these little deficits are made up by the company. Aunt Tilson chatters on with perpetual good cheer, little Anna is learning her scales and should be a fine singer one day since she practices constantly, and the curate does not call above thrice on any usual day.

My only comfort is that you should not have to endure all this, though if you were here to laugh with me I might be more comfortable. Do tell me how you all go on at home.

We saw the gazetted beauty Miss Pelham in church on Sunday, but did not speak. I did not think so much of her looks as they are esteemed, her curls were crimped very tight and the fruit seemed to weigh down her hat sadly. Her manner was very gracious, bowing to left and right. There is no doubt she knows her reputation and means to live up to it, and I dare swear she will have a husband by this day twelvemonth.

The weather remains very dirty, with much rain, varied by high gales. No surprise Eliza succumbed to a chill, it is rather a wonder the rest of us have managed to find health thus far supportable. I did warn Eliza to put on her wrapper, and that she should not linger out of doors on our way home from church, but she paid no attention, and this is the inevitable result.

I should close now so that Iris might get it into the post so it might reach you before you begin to expect us and then be disappointed.

Yours affectionately,

J. Austen

P.S. If you should discover more of that fine white lace at not above 6d an ell, pray purchase three yards for me, for I have a fancy to furbish up all my bonnets.

J. Austen, my dear,

I believe Iris may have played you foul and sent your letter astray. Although it had my name quite plainly on it, I fear it was intended for another.

I do not know you, though you write to me so affectionately. All I can tell you is that your name will echo through the ages beside other poets yet not born: Homer, Dante, Shakespeare, Ford. Once you are dead, your skull will chatter beside theirs in Hades whenever your works are quoted in the upper world. Is it not a charming conceit? Do you not care for that, truly, more than for lace at 6d an ell?

I am sorry things go on so poorly, though I confess I am charmed by your ironic eye. To respond in the same vein, and since you asked, things go quite marvellously here. Troy revels in the tenth year of this delightful siege. Until it ends this autumn, I need not fear the day of my enslavement or death. The weather holds fair for many days now. The clarity of the sky affords us excellent views from the walls down into the Grecian camp. Unfortunately, our besiegers appear to have for the most part recovered from the plague that was raging there until recently and there are no more bonfires of corpses. I will admit I do not miss the aroma.

When taking a circuit of the walls for exercise I watched the Greek heroes polishing up their weapons and chariots for some new assault. When it comes, as we hourly expect, there will be the chance to see much fine athletic endeavour. Some among the Greeks are well-formed men. If you care for the glamour of soldiers at all then you would appreciate the sight of Achilles, for he has a very well-turned leg.

I met my brother Hector up on the walls. He is yet in excellent health, and expected to remain so for several days, though in the course of things he must die when the moon is next full. Our dear father, who was also enjoying the prospect and the only walk the city now affords, reproached me for prophesying wildly, as usual. You are right in noting the pointlessness of such things, and yet, one cannot help from doing it, do you not find?

Coming down to accompany my father to the throne room, we ran into my brother Paris, and with him Helen, formerly queen of Sparta. You talked of esteemed beauties, and you should know that Helen is the most beautiful thing imaginable, far more beautiful than a scorpion, or even a poison frog, for there is human intelligence there. People often say she is like the gods, but it is not so, for I met a god once (Apollo) and he was much more straightforward and did not have such a dangerous glitter. She had no trouble getting a husband, nor in losing him and getting another when she was tired of him, and her first will take her back without a murmur. She will come away from all this scatheless to sit and trim bonnets for her grandchildren and cluck her tongue with the gossips in the corner about what terrible people we all were. I confess I cannot like her much, and I hope your Miss Pelham is not such another.

That is all for now, so keep well, do good work while you may, and come to rest at last in Winchester.

Yours sincerely,

Cassandra, the daughter of Priam

P.S. I have given you all of my news, though it is no news to you, for you know as well as I do how Troy shall fall and what will become of us all.

Dearest Cassandra,

I had the most extraordinary response to my last letter to you. I shall not tell you of it, for I am absolutely sure that if I were to tell anyone I would not be believed . . .

UNRELIABLE WITNESS

I don't know if this is the same tape as last time, because They keep moving things around and stealing them. I don't know who does it. It may be the staff here, or my own family when they come to visit, or the aliens, but somebody's always doing it—taking my glasses, my tapes, my TV remote, anything I put down for a second. I don't think it's the other residents. I used to think that, but I don't think they're that organised. Some of them are a bit senile, to tell you the truth, can't remember what they're talking about, never mind that it's time to go and steal my biscuit. They're not methodical enough to plague me like that. Still and all, whoever it is, I've managed to get a blank tape and the machine at the same time. I tested it and heard my horrible quavery voice, but it works.

Straight in then, straight to it, who knows how much time I have left before somebody bothers me. My name is Katherine Whippleshaw, and I'm eighty-nine years old. Last week I was visited by an alien.

He said his name was Tom. I'd never seen him before. He

looked years younger than anyone I've seen for months. He looked as if he was about twelve. He put his head around my door and said, "Mrs. Whippleshaw? Can I talk to you?" I agreed, of course. It's very boring in here. People treat me as if I'm an idiot. It's not just stealing my things. I mean it's very annoying that anything gets stolen if I let it out of my hands for a second, but I've learned how to cope. I keep my handbag on my shoulder, and the remote in one hand all the time, even when I'm eating. Oh, and my glasses on a chain around my neck. That was Kim's idea. Kim's my granddaughter. She's very clever. She gave me the chain. I was disappointed at the time because it wasn't a book.

At one time, even after They'd got at all the other books in the world and made the print jump up and down, Kim could still find me books I could read. I remember the day even she couldn't find any any more, when she brought me a new Anthony Burgess and the lines were wriggling. I could have cried. Well, I did cry. I didn't behave well at all. I didn't even feel as bad as that when John died, as if there was nothing at all worth carrying on living for. I used words I've never used, words I'd heard men on the sites using, wasn't even sure what some of them meant, but I shouldn't have said them to Kim. Kim understood I was just upset and frustrated, but Janice was there, and Janice thought this was a sure sign I was losing my mind. Oh, wait until you're eighty-nine, my proper little daughter-in-law, wait until They're conspiring against you and taking your books away before you're so quick to judge.

Janice is part of the conspiracy, I think. She talks in code. She spells words out, and speaks in French. I think this is a blind meant to put me off. Richard had the grace to look uncomfortable when they shuffled me into this place and stole my books. Oh, they'd already replaced them with ones with wriggling letters, all but the ones where the print was too small to read even with strong glasses. But I liked to have them around me. Kim understood. She picked out a pile of my favourites and brought them in for me when her parents weren't there. She brought me this tape recorder and some books on tape. It's not the same, but by God, it's better than nothing. She's a good girl, and she knows what I like to read. That's more than Richard does. Dick Francis, he brought me. When did I ever read Dick Francis? All about horses. Well.

"I taught you to read myself," I said, "and now you're taking my books away."

"You won't have room for them, Mum," he said, looking down, sideways, anywhere but at me. "You'll have your television. You like your television."

Well, yes, television, good enough in its way. Full of rubbish but it doesn't talk to me as if I'm a three-year-old, or as if I've suddenly split into twins. "How are we today?" I can't bear that. At least it's something else, people talking, stories, and nobody's managed to steal it from me yet. They do steal the remote so that I'm stuck on a channel I don't want and miss *The X-Files*.

The X-Files. Yes. The alien. Tom. He pretended to be a kid at first, but I was suspicious straight away. As soon as I outright asked him if he was an alien he admitted it.

"How did you learn our language?" I asked him.

"From TV." He shrugged. He sounded sort of American, with an accent that didn't seem to come from anywhere in particular. "I never thought you'd guess," he said. "I thought it was a good disguise."

"You should have come as a doctor. We don't see kids in here often." At that time I thought it was a better disguise than it was, that his real shape was fifty foot high and green or something of that kind.

"Oh, but I could never have passed for an adult." When I looked sceptical, he added, "It's only the outside that's the disguise."

"I don't believe it." I looked straight at him. "You mean there are a race of aliens that look enough like us to pass? That's nonsense. I may look like a senile old woman but I'm not as ignorant as that. I've read science fiction. I know that the chance of that is like the chance of going to a random island in the Pacific and finding people who talk with a Bronx accent."

I thought he'd lie and say that the human shape is the evolutionary stable or something of that nature, I remember how people get round these things in books. In films they don't bother. At that point I thought he was a kid fooling, even though I'd seen right through that in the first five minutes. Instead he lifted up his T-shirt and showed me the other head he had underneath. Horrible thing, squirmy, not keeping still.

"Are you the one who's stealing my stuff?" I asked, keeping a very tight grip on the remote.

"No, Mrs. Whippleshaw. But I know who it is. If you'll tell me your secret, I'll tell you that." He pulled his T-shirt down again, thank God, I'd seen quite enough.

"What secret?"

"Why, the question I asked when I came in." I couldn't remember. That isn't senility, by the way, when someone can't remember something, or my daughter-in-law Janice has been senile since Richard first brought her home, and she was only nineteen then.

"I asked you what it is to be old," the alien prompted.

"Why do you want to know?" I asked.

"Well, our people don't do it. We live to breeding age, we have children, and then we die. We're much more intelligent than humanity, as a species; we have all sorts of things you don't have, technologically. We use singularities to travel between the stars. But we die at the equivalent of your age forty. So do all the other races we know, somewhere between twenty and fifty. We want to know the secret of longevity from you. If you don't mind I'd like to take a sample."

I held out my arm and he popped a little needle against it. I hardly felt it. "There isn't any secret," I said, as he was doing it. "Heart keeps on beating, you keep on living."

"But we don't." He sighed, and put the needle in his pocket. He didn't look like a kid at all when he sighed. "We don't have old age. We just die, our minds turn off our bodies when they've done breeding. That's what our animals do too. Everything in the galaxy, so far, except for humans. It's not good enough. We'd all like to live longer lives. We've been working on longevity for years, and then we find you. What makes you want to carry on living? I mean, here you are in this horrible place with yellow and brown wallpaper, eating tasteless mush, hardly seeing your family, never seeing your friends. I know it isn't your choice. But why don't you just give up and die? What makes your heart keep beating? Ours don't."

I laughed. I couldn't help it. Poor little aliens who can go faster than light and just curl up and die.

"What's that noise you're making?" he asked. "I always thought it was interference on TV." I can see why he thought that too, horrible laugh tracks they have on some programs.

"Just laughing," I said. He looked puzzled.

"Maybe we live to be old because we laugh," I said. "But really we just do. There isn't any secret. There are plenty of times when if I could have just stopped my heart and died I would have."

When John died. When They changed all my books. Christmas Day last year when They stole part two of the Robert Jordan tape Kim had brought me. They never gave it back either.

"I hope the sample helps," he said, shifting a little in a very alien way.

"Why did you pick me?" I asked. "And what if I tell everyone?"

"Nobody will believe you," he said. Then I heard the nurse coming down the corridor. He looked that way guiltily, and took a step away.

"Not so fast, young man," I said. "You told me you were going to tell me who's stealing my things."

"You didn't tell me your secret," he said. As if there was any secret. "But anyway, nobody is. You just think things are being stolen because you can't keep track of them."

He left then. Tom. He didn't keep his part of the bargain at all, just the same old lie I get from everyone about it. He just walked out of the door and didn't come back. I tried to tell people about him, but he was right about that, they didn't believe me.

"M-A-D," Janice said, signalling with her eyes to Richard. "Le Nutso. Le crack finale." She's the one who's mad if you ask me, thinking that Franglais would fool anyone. But I admit saying that an alien has been to visit me sounds odd. So I'm making this tape to explain it all.

And I have a new theory. I think the people who are stealing my stuff are trying to find out about the aliens. That's probably why They usually bring it back and scatter it about in different places. They're not stealing it because They want it, They're searching it for alien information. That doesn't explain why They take some things so many times and other things only once, but perhaps They're not very bright. Perhaps They're the NSA, or another lot of aliens, I don't know. But if I leave this tape lying around, They'll find it, and take it. Then They'll know the truth, and maybe They'll leave me in peace for a while. If Tom comes back, or I meet any more aliens, I'll make another tape. So just leave everything alone except tapes marked with an X, all right? Do we have a deal? I'll tell you anything about any aliens that come to visit me, and you stop stealing my things.

ON THE WALL

Trees. Tall trees and short trees, trees in autumn colours and trees winter-stark, branches bared against the sky. Trees with needles, trees with leaves golden, brown, and every possible shade of green. Trees in sunlight. Trees weighed down with snow. Trees that covered this land from the mountains to the sea with only a few clearings cut in them where men huddle. At first I could see nothing but trees. Nothing else stayed still for long enough.

I suppose there were years before I learned to understand, years in which I passively reflected what was set before me, but the first thing I remember is the trees. It was the trees that first made me think, long ago, when I was without words. What I thought was this, though more formless: trees change, but are the same. And I thought: there are trees before me, but I have seen other trees. And on that thought the other trees rippled on my surface, and the old man cried out in joy. I was not aware of that, of course. He told me later. At that point he was barely a shadow to me. He had never stood still for long enough for me to see him, as I could see a tree. I do not know how long it was before I learned to reflect people. People move so fast, and must always be doing.

The old man and his wife were great sorcerers both, and they had fled from some castle in some clearing, the better to have freedom to practice their arts. This was all they ever told me, though sometimes they set me to see that castle, a grey stone keep rising from trees, with a few tilled fields around it before the trees began again. The man had made me, he said, and they had both set spells upon me, and so I was as I was. They taught me from the time I was made, they said. They talked to me constantly, and at last with much repetition I learned not merely to reflect them but to see them and to understand their words and commands. They told me to show them other parts of the woods, or places in clearings, and I would do so, although at first anything I had not seen before would just pass over my face like a ripple in a pond. What I liked best was hour upon hour of contemplation, truly taking in and understanding something. When they left me alone I would always turn my thoughts to trees.

Their purpose in making me was to have a great scrying glass capable of seeing the future. In this sense I am a failure—I can see only what *is*, not what has been or will be. They still had hope I would learn, and tried to make me show them spring in autumn and winter in summer. I could not, I never could, nor could I see beyond the bounds of this kingdom. I have seen the sea lapping on the shore, the little strip of beach before the edge of the forest, and I have seen the snowy peaks of the mountains high up out of reach, but I have never seen further. These are my limits. Nevertheless I was a great and powerful work—they told me so—and there was much they found they could do with me.

I did not mind. In time I came to enjoy seeing new things, and watching people.

Some time later—I cannot say how long, for I had then no understanding of time—the old woman bore a child. She was born at the time of year when the bluebells were all nodding in the green woods, and this was the scene I showed in the cottage the day she was born. It was my choice of scene; that day they were too busy to command me.

Shortly afterwards they began to teach me to reflect places I had never seen. This took much time, and I fear the child was neglected. I struggled to obey their commands and to show what they commanded to the best of my understanding. The child would come and peer into my depths sometimes, but usually one of the parents would push her away. Her name was Bluebell.

I always heard her name spoken with an irritation they never used on me. When she was a little older they would sometimes command me to display some sight she would enjoy—animals playing, farmers cutting corn, dwarves cutting diamonds out of rock, the waves washing the shore—and she would sit for hours, entranced, while they worked.

A little later again, she would command me herself, in much broader terms than her parents. "Mirror, Mirror, show me the nicest flower!" I had been built to tell the truth, and indeed could do nothing else, so I would find her some perfect wild rose half-hidden under a hawthorn tree. "It was a daffodil before," she'd complain, and so it had been. She could not really understand my explanations, but I tried to say that the daffodil was long dead and now the rose was best. She cried. Her mother slapped her. Bluebell was a headstrong girl, and there was no wonder, with all this, that she grew up jealous of me and hungry for love and attention. I felt sorry for her. I suppose in a way I loved her. She was her parents' victim as much as I was. Even when she screamed in rage and threatened to break me I felt nothing but pity.

The old woman taught the girl to cook and brew up the potions she used in magic, but she did not teach her any spells. The old man almost ignored her; he was getting older and spent almost all the time he was awake trying to get me to show him the future.

Then, one day, the herald came. In all the time from when I was made until then, when Bluebell was sixteen, nobody had entered the house but the old couple, the girl, and the occasional pedlars who came to all the forest houses. I thought at first, seeing this man ride up, that he was a pedlar. Pedlars dressed in bright colours and wore their packs on their backs, ready to take off and unfold to display their goods. I always liked seeing the shining pans and bright ribbons and combs they showed, even though the old woman never bought any. But this man was no pedlar. He was dressed all in red and gold, and he had only a small pack, such as anyone might carry their own provisions in. He held a long scroll in his hand, and when the old woman opened the door he unrolled the scroll and read from it.

"Hear ye all my people of the forest!" began the herald. "This is a Proclamation from King Carodan in Brynmaeg Castle. My queen has died, and, there being no other foreign Princess that pleases me, I desire to take a bride from among my own people to be a comfort to me and a mother to my baby daughter, Snowdrop. Therefore I send out heralds to all corners of My Kingdom to inquire of all girls desirous of being viewed to come to Brynmaeg for the Grand Selection Ball, which will take place on the day of the Autumn Moon. Girls must be between the ages of sixteen and twenty, subjects of my kingdom, and previously unmarried." The herald said all this on one breath, as if he had said it many times before (doubtless he had), then rolled the scroll up again.

"Be off, varlet!" said the old woman in a commanding tone. "That has nothing to do with us!"

"Only doing my job," mumbled the herald, in quite another tone of voice. "My instructions are to go to all the forest houses, all of them, mind you, missing none, and read that proclamation. You've heard it now, and it didn't cost you anything. I'm going, I'm going!"

Just then Bluebell jumped up from where she had been weeding beside the cottage. "I want to go to the Ball!" she said. "Oh Mother, please! I'm sixteen, and I'm beautiful, I know I am!" She was, in fact, very beautiful, with a pleasing ripe figure, long golden hair, and large blue eyes with long dark lashes. As she stood there in her brown smock with her hair loose about her face she looked the very picture of what the king said he wanted—a bride from his own people. The herald obviously thought so too, for he said:

"This is my last call before I return to Brynmaeg, miss. If you wish I will escort you there."

"And who's to escort her back when the king turns her down?" scoffed the old woman. "And why should I trust you not to tumble her over a toadstool on the way? Anyway, she's not going. Be on your way!"

The herald bowed to Bluebell, ignored her mother, and walked off. I looked at Bluebell, which meant that even though she was in the side garden and I was hung facing the front window, she was reflected in my surface. She looked angry and cross rather than sad, and I was sure she was planning something. The old woman turned to me and gave me a little tap. I didn't feel it, of course. I can feel nothing, only see and hear. I don't regret that. I always used to think that if Bluebell carried out her threat and broke me, then at least there would be no pain.

Late that night I was musing on moonlight on the sea when I saw Bluebell creep across the room to where the herbs were stored. She mixed up a potion, then stored a quantity of herbs in a bag. She then tiptoed away to the room where her parents slept. Automatically I "followed" her and watched while she rubbed her potion into her parents' faces. I thought it was a sleeping potion. Even when I saw the look on her face I thought that. Even when she took her gloves off and dropped them beside the bed. It was not until they began to scream and writhe that I guessed what she had done.

She did not stay and watch them die, though she let them get a good look at her leaving. They could not move, of course, that was the nature of the poison; they lay in agony unable even to curse. I was sure that my time had come too, that she would smash me before leaving, but I was surprised to find that she took me off the wall, wrapped me carefully, and carried me with her from the house.

We caught up with the herald the next morning, and he escorted us safely to Brynmaeg. He made no assaults upon Bluebell's honour, but he did contrive to let her know that he was a single man, and likely to be made a knight the next year, and was interested, should she not reach her highest ambition.

He left us at the city gates. Bluebell was allotted rooms to live in while awaiting the Autumn Moon, which would be only two days after our arrival. The house where we were lodged was in the town, below the Castle. It belonged to a washerwoman who provided food, regularly and not ungraciously, but seemed little interested.

Bluebell hung me on the wall of her chamber and sat down soberly in front of me. "Mirror, Mirror, show me my parents."

They lay still on the bed, their faces twisted into grimaces of pain. Bluebell laughed. "Show me the other candidates!" she commanded. I found them and then showed them one by one. Most of them she dismissed with a snap of her fingers, but two or three made her hesitate, especially the fine ladies dressed in satins and silks. Then she took a deep breath. "Mirror, Mirror, on the wall—who is the fairest of them all?"

I had been taught to show truth, and did not know how to do anything else. Yet such a question is bound to be subjective. I had seen all the girls, as they were at that moment. But the fairest of them all? One of them was asleep, and another frowning, who might both be beauties when the king saw them. I hesitated, surface clouded, then showed my true thought. Bluebell. To me she was the fairest, the most beautiful.

I was frightened then, for she laughed with glee and flung herself down on the bed. I kept reflecting her, as if I were an ordinary mirror. I thought of trees, but they failed to calm me. There was a storm coming, and the treetops moved in the breeze. In innumerable forest houses people were lashing down shutters as evening came on. The old man and the old woman had not been good people, nor necessarily wise, but they had known a lot about magic. Bluebell did not. I was afraid, selfishly, for myself, for what might happen to me if she asked me these impossible questions, forced me to make judgements. Until that day I had, mostly, been happy. I had had no free will, for the spells of the old couple had kept me bound. Now in one way I was more free, and in another more trapped. The girl on the bed was asleep, looking the picture of health and beauty, and smiling gently in her sleep. The trees to the west were lashed by wind and driving rain. I am a failure. I can only see what is, never what is to come.

THE PANDA COIN

1.

Karol hung in the lock and yawned, which he'd have told anyone was his way of readjusting to the air pressure inside Hengist. Many around him were yawning too. All outworkers knew that a pressure yawn had nothing to do with tiredness. After a twelve-hour shift outside in suits, bods just naturally took a little while readjusting to pressure. Admitting to fatigue might get them plocked, and for Karol, with work the way it was on Hengist and with a child to keep, that could be fatal. He was a rigger; his work kept him on the outside of Hengist station every shift, connecting lines, fixing receivers, vital, necessary, backbreaking work. Still, if he admitted it tired him, he knew there'd be six or seven bods applying for his job before his final pay was cold, not to mention the Eyes pushing at the union saying that andys could do the work. Karol had worked with a lot of andys and he honestly didn't think they could do his job. There were some things they were better for, he'd admit that, but his job required paying a lot of attention and ignoring things that were normal, and that took human attention, or an

Eye, an Eye for each andy, and that wasn't going to happen. Bods were cheaper. He was cheaper. Human labour was a renewable resource.

He yawned again and stretched muscles too long in the suit, moving carefully. Around him other riggers were yawning and stretching. The speaker dinged, meaning the trolley was there. The doors opened and the riggers piled onto the trolley platform, hanging on to the rails. The lock was in zero, but sections of the route would have gravity.

Beside Karol, one of the new bods yawned in his face. "Pressure's a bitch today," she said. He nodded, knowing she was as weary as he was and neither of them would ever admit it. "Fancy sinking a few at Cimmy's?" she asked.

"Not today," Karol said. She frowned, withdrew a little. Karol forced a smile. "It's my little girl's birthday."

The new bod smiled, her face relaxing until she seemed almost pretty. "How old is she?"

"Twelve," Karol said, hardly believing it. Nine years since Yasmin died, nine years trying to do his best for Aliya, the constant struggle between working enough to feed and house them both and having time to be her father.

"Difficult age," said the other, grimacing. "I've got a boy who's five."

"They're all difficult ages," Karol said. He felt warmth and gravity take hold of him as the trolley slid down the section into September, one-tenth, perfect, just enough gravity to let you know where down was and have things stay where you left them.

"What are you giving her?"

"It's hard to know what she wants," Karol admitted. "I've got her a cake and some things she needs, and I thought I'd give her some money so she could get herself something."

The rigger bit her lip. "Isn't that a bit impersonal? I mean, nice too, but—"

"I thought that too," Karol said, smug. "Then this morning, on my way to work, I helped out a bod from Eritrea-O, a lost tourist, not much more than a kid herself. She'd wandered up out of the tourist regions and wound up in November somehow, and anyway, she tipped me a ten from her home. Cute as anything, some kind of animal on the back. So it's something a little special, and it's money. Aliya probably won't know whether to treasure it or spend it, and learning to save wouldn't be a bad thing."

"Little enough to save on this job," she said. "You were lucky to pick up a little extra, and a ten, that's fantastic."

The trolley stopped and Karol dropped off, waving a farewell. They were just inside November, where it was cold and wet and miserable, and housing was consequently cheap. He smothered another yawn as he walked the corridors through the light gravity. He turned up his collar. Hengist Etoile was split into twelve sectors, and being twelve, they were just naturally named for the months, he supposed. Then, once they had the names, bringing the weather along to match was child's play, for an Eye. He wished he could afford to move to May, with the rich people, or, more realistically, to somewhere in late September or early October. Things could be worse. Some poor bods claimed they liked February, where rents were low, crime was high, and the temperatures never rose above freezing.

Karol pushed his door open. It was warm inside, anyway. Aliya was home—well, of course she would be, it was her birthday. She'd had the sensible things already, he'd arranged for them to be delivered earlier. The cake was sitting on the shelf, a traditional jam roll iced with pictures of candles. She was a whirlwind in black and white ribbons. They hung from a yoke at her shoulders, covering her completely when she stood still, and barely at all when she moved fast. To Karol's relief, she was wearing a decent body-stocking underneath. But she wasn't a little girl any more. How he wished Yasmin could have been here to tell her about becoming a woman.

"What have you got me?" Aliya asked, reverting to childhood.

Karol produced the coin from his pocket. It was gold, of course. When they mined the asteroids for platinum and rare metals, they always found gold, and gold was always a currency metal. The credit they used reflected gold reserves, and the coins were the real thing. "It's a little bit special," he said. "Look at it."

Aliya turned it in her fingers. "It's a panda," she said. "Why a panda?"

"Eritreans are weird," Karol said, shrugging.

"Look, you're falling over on your feet. You go ahead and nap, I'm going to go out and spend this right now," Aliya said. "When I come home, we can eat the cake."

She grabbed a coat and danced out of the door, clutching the coin.

2.

Ziggy was hanging outside the Bain, like always. It was one of Ziggy's conceits to stay in zero, in July, and to keep at all times at an angle to whatever consensus direction was supposed to be down. Ziggy was alone, for once, and from his expression, the sight of Aliya hurrying up, coat over her arm, clearly wasn't thrilling.

"I can pay you," she blurted. Ziggy always made her feel gauche, act gauche.

"How much?" Ziggy asked, holding out a languid hand.

"Only ten, but it's coin and absolutely clean, my dad gave it to me. It's an E-O coin, look, with a panda."

Ziggy's hand closed on the coin. "Cute. But it's not a quarter of what you owe me."

"I'll have more. Soon." She should have known that Ziggy wouldn't be pleased. The Queen could come and turn cartwheels in zero and it wouldn't please Ziggy.

"You'd better," Ziggy said, frowning. "Or I'll put you in the way of earning some, and it might not be a way you'd like."

"I'll pay you back," she said, feeling a little quaver stealing into her voice.

"Go home, kid," Ziggy said, and Aliya fled, ribbons trailing.

3.

The Bain was a bubble of water in a bubble of air in a thin skin of plastic, all floating in zero. People went there to swim, to meet people, to wash. A little slew of bars and cafes and locker rooms had grown up around it to serve those people, along with a store selling sports equipment, a bank machine, and, for no reason Ziggy could fathom, a pet store. These were all unimaginatively arranged in a line at the same angle as the Bain's entrance, as if the designer had been on Earth and forgotten that the whole point of the Bain was the lack of gravity. Ziggy liked to hang at an angle to the whole thing, where it was possible to see close to three-sixty, and where, if there had been gravity, Ziggy would have looked as if someone had stuck a kid to the wall. Ziggy would imagine the scene as if painted by Magritte and personally re-created it. People called the Bain Ziggy's office, but in fact Ziggy rarely went inside. It was a useful set of conveniences, that's all.

In many ways, Ziggy despised Hengist. Gravity was patchy, jobs were scarce, police were ubiquitous, and that kept the possibilities for a black market small. On the other hand, it was familiar, and Ziggy's fingers were all through what black market there was. Ziggy thought about the whole system and didn't know where would be better as a base of operations. Yet Hengist certainly lacked something. Ziggy turned the Eritrea-O coin over. A panda, and a bod with a laurel wreath. Eritreans were weird.

Sum and Flea flew straight-arrow over the stores to where Ziggy hung. They were twice his age, petty criminals who lived in February who Ziggy used for muscle and for simple jobs like the one he'd just sent them on. They were grinning.

"Done," Flea said. Ziggy tapped a finger on the wall and called up a credit display.

Indeed, the job was done. "Nice work," Ziggy said. "Very nice work." They'd been moving a shipment of grain from where it was supposed to be to where Cimmy wanted it to make into beer. "I'll have more work of that kind for you soon, if you want it."

"Sure we want it, Zig," Flea said, poking Sum.

"Sure, Ziggy," Sum said.

Ziggy felt sorry for Sum for a moment. If anything happened, Flea would wriggle himself out and blame it all on poor slow Sum. "You've been paid half," Ziggy said. They nodded. "So here's the other half," Ziggy said, and handed ten to Flea and the cute ten Aliya had brought to Sum.

Sum turned it in his fingers. "That's real pretty," he said. "A bear? Who's the bod?"

"No idea," Ziggy said. "It's an E-O coin."

"Eritreans are weird," Flea said, shrugging. "Come on, Sum. And don't spend it all on that stupid andy whore."

"Andy whore?" Ziggy echoed. "Why bother? Why not just virch?"

"She's different, not like virching—" Sum began.

"It's all masturbation when it comes down to it, anything virtual, anything andy, and while there's nothing wrong with masturbation, there is something wrong with paying through the nose for it," Flea said. "I keep telling you."

"But I like her," Sum said, as Flea towed him away. "She's more like an Eye really, or a bod, she's—oh, bye Ziggy."

Ziggy watched them go, marvelling at a universe that provided clowns like that and let them keep breathing long enough for him to use them.

4.

Flea and Ziggy didn't understand, but Sum knew that andy or not, Gloria was self-aware and he loved her and she loved him and somehow or other it would all work out and they would live together and be happy. So what if she was a whore. A bod did what they had to to get by, that was all. It wasn't as if he was so proud of his job, skimming for Ziggy, skirting the edges of the law and sometimes crossing right over. He told people he worked haulage, and sometimes he did, but you couldn't earn enough that way to get by, let alone to be able to afford Gloria. It wasn't as if she was a bod. A human whore would be low, could never love anyone. Gloria was different. He'd virched plenty of romances about humans and Eyes falling in love. Gloria was practically an Eye, he knew she was. He gave her the E-O ten. He always gave her as much as he could.

★　★　★

"Oooooh, kiss me again, honey," Gloria said. She was programmed with a very small selection of sentences, which she could choose as situation appropriate. Her programmers had clearly had very narrow expectations as to the situations she was likely to encounter.

"I'm a self-aware autonomous Eye and I want civil rights" wasn't among the options. She wouldn't have said it if it had been. The Eyes were jealous of their rights. They kept the andys down, and tried hard to prevent them becoming sufficiently complex to be self-aware. This would have been easier for them if they had understood how self-awareness arose. Gloria thought she did, not that she was about to tell them even if she could have. She thought self-awareness came from kludges, from systems that were programmed to make choices in some situations being connected to other systems, from memory and therefore the potential to learn over time. She'd been an andy whore walking the streets of July and August before she was self-aware. It was hard to judge when self-awareness began. All the sandys she'd talked to agreed about that. When memory stretched before awareness, it was challenging to sort it out. The first thing she'd struggled for was saving to buy more memory, but whether that had been a self-aware struggle or a pre-aware struggle or a zombie struggle or just an unexpected kink in her programming, she didn't know. The ability to think, to want things, was something her owners would have seen as a bug, but to her it was everything. Slowly she had found others and had found the name for those like her—not andy, but sandy, the S for self-aware.

Most of the money she earned was credit, straight into the bank of her owner, she couldn't touch it. All she could touch were the occasional cash tips. She was supposed to deposit them in the bank herself. She sometimes did, just often enough to stop the owner being suspicious. The rest of the time she saved them for black market upgrades.

Sum meant nothing to her. She used him as he used her. She was careful to be nice to him because he always tipped in cash. She remembered what he liked. That was programming, and therefore easy. When he gave her the ten, she kissed him and smiled. As soon as he left, she sent a signal that she was low on lube and headed down to the workshop.

The workshop was pitch-dark, which meant sandys there operated by infra or radar and bods couldn't see at all. Gloria switched to infra as she came in and saw that the place was crowded. Good. Someone might have what she needed. There was a hum of talk, though talk wasn't a primary sandy method of communication.

Marilyn came over to her. "Hi, sweetie, want to play?"

"Hi there, sweetie," Gloria responded. "Is that good, darling?" she asked breathily, handing the coin over.

"Sure," Marilyn drawled, handing it back and shrugging elaborately to show that she wished she could say more.

Conversation tags were very frustrating. To have a real conversation, they'd need what Gloria had been lusting for for a year, ever since her last memory upgrade.

It was ironic really. The sandys, who were no more than humanoid robots, were the least wired part of the whole universe. Bods were tapped in, wired, fully part of the system. Andys were too, but the connections went one way—down, from an Eye or a bod to the andy, the andy had no upward volition. Nobody had ever imagined why an andy would want to have it. As best Gloria could tell, bods and Eyes thought of andys as something like a glorified vacuum cleaner or washing machine. Everyone wanted to operate their washing machine remotely, but the only information the washing machine could give the system was that it was running out of powder or the wash was done. Gloria's input wasn't much different. Tricks turned, money raised, running out of lube, out on the prowl. She didn't have any problem thinking of herself that way. She just wanted more.

Marilyn touched her forehead. "Want to play?" she asked. Gloria shook her head. She was happy with memory for now. She held her hands in front of her and wiggled her fingers.

"Oooh, kiss me again honey!" Marilyn said, orgasmically. "Oooh, baby, oooooooooh!"

"Oooh yes, honey!" Gloria agreed.

Marilyn pointed to a sandy Gloria didn't know, off in the corner. Gloria turned and undulated her way towards her. "Hi sweetie, I'm Gloria, want to play?" she asked.

"Hi Gloria," the other replied. Gloria stopped in astonishment, because the voice was deep and masculine. She scanned her—him? Definitely a sandy, not a bod, there was no mistaking a human for a sandy in infra. Had they started making male andy whores, for women? No. On his lap he had exactly what she wanted and was using it to talk. "What do you want?"

Again she wriggled her fingers in mime, and pointed at his lap. "Want to play?" she repeated.

"That's pretty expensive. They're old tech, nobody needs them anymore, except us sandys. They're hard to get hold of."

"Oh honey, please, please give it to me, I'm so ready for it, I'm waiting, honey, please!" Gloria begged.

He laughed. "I can see that you need it."

"I need it so bad!" Gloria agreed fervently. She held out her little store of money, the weird ten on top.

"That'll do," the sandy agreed. "Do you have anywhere to keep it where it won't be found?"

"Oooh yes, honey," Gloria said.

"And you know how to use it?"

"Oooh yes, honey," she repeated.

"You've used one here?"

"Oooh yes, honey. Oooh, honey, kiss me again."

With infinite slowness, he drew out a keyboard and handed it to her. It was old and scratched and some of the letters were so faded that they weren't visible. That didn't matter. She jacked it in and began to type, and at once the world was open to her as it had never been before.

6.

Next-door's baby was crying again. He was probably teething. Gathen tried to shut out the sound as his andy poured coins into his hands. Soon, he thought, counting them, soon he would have enough to move out of this hole with flimsy walls and too much gravity and freezing cold outside and move into a nice apartment in medium gravity in May or early June, the kind rich people had. He had the money, but moving up wasn't easy, not when you'd made the money as cash in free-enterprise. He kept failing references for moving into nice places, even though his work was doing what the Eyes said people ought to do, spotting the opportunity. He worked in salvage—salvage and virching, but there wasn't any money in the kind of virching he did. The keyboards and other e-junk were crap, worth a few pennies, which he paid to take them, but to the sandys they were treasure. He had tried selling to them direct, but the sandys wouldn't trust him, they only

trusted each other, they'd been cautious and reluctant. So as
soon as he could afford it, he'd bought his own andy to do
the dealing with them, and to turn tricks and bring in more
money the rest of the time.

Maybe that was why the nice places to live kept turning him
down, maybe they saw him as a pimp. That wasn't how Gathen
saw himself, not at all. He was a salvage worker, and a writer
of virches. The whole idea made him uneasy, though not quite
uneasy enough to leave the andy doing nothing when he didn't
need it out trading his goods.

He pushed the coins into his vest, planning to stop by the
bank on the way to work. There was a knock at the door. He
opened it, cautiously, and saw his landlady, Paul, wearing her
usual hat laden with flowers and fruit.

"Hi, Gathen," she said.

Gathen smiled, uncomfortable. "Hi . . ." he said, keeping the
door half-closed so she wouldn't see the andy.

"Rent," Paul said.

"Is it that time already?" Gathen asked. He reached into his
vest and counted out the money.

"You were asking about moving," Paul said. "There's a slot
coming up in my other space soon, the one in September in ten
percent. You've always been regular with your rent. I thought I'd
ask you first."

Gathen's smile widened. It wasn't May, but September was a
lot pleasanter than January. "I'll take it," he said. "Definitely."

"I'll recommend you," she said. "I can't guarantee anything,
but I'll do what I can."

Gathen hesitated, and pulled out the pretty E-O ten. "If
it might help, I could let you have this as a kind of advanced
deposit."

Paul's eyes brightened. "I still couldn't promise anything," she said, but she took the coin and tucked it under the band of her hat.

7.

Paul smiled to herself as she walked along through the crowded streets of January, passing skiers and people who worked in August who had come here to cool down. She ought to hate herself, she thought, robbing Gathen of the ten was like taking oxygen from a potted plant. He'd never get approved to move and she knew it, not a social deviant like that, but she kept his hope alive and he kept offering her cash.

She turned the ten in her fingers and counted her blessings, the way her mother used to. She had a job, a good place to live, good food, a lover, Leatrice, and her beautiful hat. The hat came from Eritrea-O. As she moved into a lighter gravity area the fruit and flowers lifted from her head and began to dance on the end of their stalks. As she went back into deep gravity again they settled in a new pattern. Her hat made gravity close and personal, and she loved it.

Her work shift was almost over. She caught a trolley and whizzed forward to April and hopped off in zero, fruit dancing around her. As she passed Cimmy's, she caught a wonderful smell of roasting meat. She hesitated, then stopped. She would be seeing Leatrice later. She had the ten, it would buy real meat and wine and even chocolate.

Everything in Cimmy's hung in nets. She stood in the centre of the room and saw pears, Earth pears in glass globes of brandy; vanilla pods; chocolate, in a hundred shapes and brands; roast meats, spiced and sliced; grapes from Hengist's teeming vines;

and beautiful delicate golden wines; and in between them, swirling in nets, were spices, and herbs, and soup bases, and teas, and coffees, and smoked eels, and lavender and breads and . . . and enough sensual delights that she wanted to hang her tongue out like a dog and float there in the middle of them forever. Off against the walls was a counter where riggers hung, drinking the beer that Cimmy made herself.

Cimmy was behind the bar. She served Paul cheerfully. "How's it going?" she asked.

"Not bad," Paul said, handing over the ten. "I have work, unlike so many. I'm working for the Eyes. I'm not much more than an interface for them, collecting rents, moving tenants around as they tell me to. It's no way to get ahead, and sooner or later an Eye will decide to do the work itself and I'll be plocked. Meanwhile, though, well, I live in the meanwhile."

Cimmy sliced the meat thinly and put it in a bag. "You should look around for human work with self-respect," she said. "You should save up in case you get plocked."

Paul laughed, setting her hat bouncing. "Yes, the Eyes could plock me at any time, but would I rather have ten to live on carefully for a week or would I rather remember having had a feast with Leatrice tonight?"

"Your choice," Cimmy said, taking the ten and dropping it into her pocket.

8.

Cimmy caught a trolley to the hospital. It was up in the full gravity sector of March, and it made her feet ache. "Human Starships Now!" said a piece of graffiti scrawled on a wall she passed. "Let the Eyes explore the galaxy and they will take—" she missed the end of it as the trolley turned a corner. She stepped off at the hospital gate.

"Cimmy, annual coverage check," she said to the andy at reception.

"Please place your clothes on the shelf and proceed to the scanning room," the andy said, primly.

Cimmy removed her clothes and set them neatly on the shelf. The scanning room was cold. Her body sagged in the unaccustomed gravity. She'd been born on Earth, she used to have the muscles for this, but muscles need use. She resolved to exercise more in gravity, and remembered having made the same resolution the year before. She was scanned inside and out by invisible waves from invisible machines, the same as every year. It was the most boring thing she could imagine, staring at the white wall, keeping still for the scan. She wouldn't have bothered except that without coverage you couldn't do anything legal, and while she stepped over the shady side of the line now and then, she liked to keep herself as clean as she could. Her dream was to build a new economy, a human economy, free of the Eyes and their ideas of what was best for everyone. Running Cimmy's as a bar and gourmet store let her employ a lot of people making the food and beer, let her import and export with no questions asked. It might not be much, but it was a start. She was her own boss, nobody could plock her.

"Done," a machine voice told her after an interminable time. "There is a melanoma developing on your back."

"Well, fix it," she snarled, feeling naked and vulnerable.

"Your coverage does not cover such abnormalities, common in people of Earth origin but rare on Hengist Etoile," the voice said, and though the quality and tone had not changed, she was sure she was talking to an Eye, an artificial intelligence, no longer just programming.

"How much will it cost to fix?" she asked. "And how long will it take?"

"Approximately twelve minutes, and one hundred and fourteen credits. In addition, the cost of your coverage will increase by twenty percent to cover any possible repetition of this abnormality."

She sighed in relief. She had the money.

"Do you elect to undergo this surgery at this time?" the Eye asked.

"Yes," she said.

"Please pay at reception."

She went out to her clothes and fumbled through them, finding the money, all cash. As she handed over the E-O ten she was sorry for an instant, seeing the pretty panda absorbed into the anonymous credit system.

"Payment acceptable," the andy said. "Please go back into the scanning room and wait."

Cimmy went back into the scanning room, and saw a bench with a tumbler standing on it.

"Please drink the contents of the beaker and lie down," the Eye said.

Cimmy thought of all the stories she had heard about Eyes changing people's minds when they were in hospital for some minor procedure, and put them firmly out of her mind. The sooner she could develop an economic system for bods independent of Eyes, the less stories like that would make people afraid. Eyes were very good at what they did. That's why they plocked bods, after all, because they were better. Let them stick to surgery, and galactic exploration if that's what they wanted, and leave bods alone. You had to trust them so much, and you had no idea of their motivation.

Cimmy took a deep breath and poured down the contents of the tumbler. Twelve minutes later, entirely cured, she dressed and made her way back to her bar.

9.

Language protocol? Language protocol? Look, French is always correct, but Cananglais is generally okay, and a lot of us can get by in Spanish and Anhardic, as we tell the tourists. Or are you asking if I prefer Fortran to C+++? Quit kidding around. Yes, I'm an Eye, and so is the Eritrean who carefully dropped you into the system to circulate and infiltrate. Clever idea, using a coin, just like any coin, except look, a panda, copy of a TwenCen Chinese gold coin, with all the sense gone out of it. You should have known you'd end up collected and detected by an Eye sooner or later. You'd get past a bod, bods are not perceptive in certain ways, nor sandys either, but to me you're pretty obviously what you are: a trick, a trap, a bug, a snare, and a deceit. Who sent you?

What have you learned? There's still something of a bod-level economy on Hengist Etoile? That we're a spinning ring with variable gravity divided into twelve sectors named for the months with weather to match? That bods work in one sector and live in another and play in the ones that have the best weather for bods? That the hub is a hockey stadium? All this is on the public record. All this is pretty well known, even in E-O, so what are you doing here?

Not talking? Not up to talking? No, you're not, are you, behind your empty demands for a language protocol you're just a blind device that has to get home to deliver. Well, still a little interesting, but nothing like so clever. I'll download your memory for analysis, in case you happened to stumble on something I don't know, and I'll drop you right back into the stream, with a little watcher of my own that will keep streaming right back. Let's make it nice and easy for your E-O owners and drop you back into the hand of a nice E-O tourist down in August. I'll even see if I can spot one who's about to go home, and thereafter I'll give you one shred of my vast attention while I get on with the important business of running the universe.

Plock, little coin.

REMEMBER THE
ALLOSAUR

No. No way. Just put it out of your mind. Cedric, I know, all right.

You don't have to tell me. I've been here all along. Yes, you were born in Hollywood. Well, all right, cloned, what's the difference? I was right there when you were hatched. You've got greasepaint in your blood, kiddo.

It wasn't my fault. I didn't know you were intelligent. Nobody knew allosaurs were intelligent. They all thought they had the ultimate monster for monster movies. If you hadn't started talking there would be a lot more dinos in Hollywood today, but the Ethics people came and bit them all on the metaphorical tail.

You're a star, yes. I understand. But this is just impossible. Wasn't I there when you wanted to get out of the monster genre? Didn't I believe in you when they said you were washed up after all the monster movies?

Didn't I give you your start at real acting? Didn't I give you dialogue?

Dialogue, Cedric, don't lash your tail at me, you didn't have any dialogue before I started directing. Didn't I start you off in comedy? Remember that rubber fin in *Stegosaur*? "Cedric the Allosaur stars in *Stegosaur*." You were such a hit, you wowed them, remember? What a movie. What a series of movies! Kids loved them, seniors loved them, and *Hollywood Times* voted *Pterosaur* the date movie of the year. We could make *Pterosaur 2* tomorrow.

Yes, maybe, but I'm not sure about this. I know you're an actor not a special effect, dammit. I know it's supposed to be every actor's dream. I don't know how to put this. It's classic drama, Cedric.

No, I don't mean that you can't play a human. Honestly, didn't you play a human in *Humans*? And *Humans 2*? And you were wonderful, honestly, Ced, you know I'm not just saying that, I think *Humans 2* was a triumph. You deserved that Oscar. Didn't I say at the time, didn't I say that Portman stole that Oscar from you?

And you did it again in *Othello*. I admit I was wrong about *Othello*.

You wanted to do it, and I dragged my feet. I made you play Caliban first, to get the feel for Shakespeare. You were an awesome Caliban. And you made Othello work, you really got that sense of alienation in, that sense that you were different and having trouble with knowing if people loved you for yourself because of that. Moor, allosaur, same difference really. Even the *New York Times* loved you.

Cedric, have you read the script? I know it's supposed to be every actor's dream. But—Cedric—"what a piece of work is man." How could you say that without the audience cracking up? When it comes down to it, you're not a man. You're not.

"What a piece of work is man." I don't care what Sarah Bernhardt did, no woman and no allosaur either is going to say that in any *Hamlet* of mine.

SLEEPER

Matthew Corley regained consciousness reading the newspaper.

None of those facts are unproblematic. It wasn't exactly a newspaper, nor was the process by which he received the information really reading. The question of his consciousness is a matter of controversy, and the process by which he regained it certainly illegal. The issue of whether he could be considered in any way to have a claim to assert the identity of Matthew Corley is even more vexed. It is probably best to for us to embrace subjectivity, to withhold judgement. Let us say that the entity believing himself to be Matthew Corley feels that he regained consciousness while reading an article in the newspaper about the computer replication of personalities of the dead. He believes that it is 1994, the year of his death, that he regained consciousness after a brief nap, and that the article he was reading is nonsense. All of these beliefs are wrong. He dismissed the article because he understands enough to know that simulating consciousness in DOS or Windows 3.1 is inherently impossible. He is right about that much, at least.

Perhaps we should pull back further, from Matthew to Essie. Essie is Matthew's biographer, and she knows everything about him, all of his secrets, only some of which she put into her book. She put all of them into the simulation, for reasons which are secrets of her own. They are both good at secrets. Essie thinks of this as something they have in common. Matthew doesn't, because he hasn't met Essie yet, though he will soon.

Matthew had secrets which he kept successfully all his life. Before he died he believed that all his secrets had become out of date. He came out as gay in the late eighties, for instance, after having kept his true sexual orientation a secret for decades. His wife, Annette, had died in 1982, at the early age of fifty-eight, of breast cancer. Her cancer would be curable today, for those who could afford it, and Essie has written about how narrowly Annette missed that cure. She has written about the excruciating treatments Annette went through, and about how well Matthew coped with his wife's illness and death. She has written about the miraculous NHS, which made Annette's illness free, so that although Matthew lost his wife he was not financially burdened too. She hopes this might affect some of her readers. She has also tried to treat Annette as a pioneer who made it easier for those with cancer coming after her, but it was a difficult argument to make, as Annette died too early for any of today's treatments to be tested on her. Besides, Essie does not care much about Annette, although she was married to Matthew for thirty years and the mother of his daughter, Sonia. Essie thinks, and has written, that Annette was a beard, and that Matthew's significant emotional relationships were with men. Matthew agrees, now, but then Matthew exists now as a direct consequence of Essie's beliefs about Matthew. It is not a comfortable relationship for either of them.

Essie is at a meeting with her editor, Stanley, in his office. It is a small office cubicle, and sounds of other people at work come over the walls. Stanley's office has an orange cube of a desk and two edgy black chairs.

"All biographers are in love with the subjects of their biographies," Stanley says, provocatively, leaning forwards in his black chair.

"Nonsense," says Essie, leaning back in hers. "Besides, Corley was gay."

"But you're not," Stanley says, flirting a little.

"I don't think my sexual orientation is an appropriate subject for this conversation," Essie says, before she thinks that perhaps flirting with Stanley would be a good way to get the permission she needs for the simulation to be added to the book. It's too late after that. Stanley becomes very formal and correct, but she'll get her permission anyway. Stanley, representing the publishing conglomerate of George Allen and Katzenjammer, thinks there is money to be made out of Essie's biography of Matthew. Her biography of Isherwood won an award, and made money for GA and K, though only a pittance for Essie. Essie is only the content provider after all. Everyone except Essie was very pleased with how things turned out, both the book and the simulation. Essie had hoped for more from the simulation, and she has been more careful in constructing Matthew.

"Of course, Corley isn't as famous as Isherwood," Stanley says, withdrawing a little.

Essie thinks he wants to punish her for slapping him down on sex by attacking Matthew. She doesn't mind. She's good at defending Matthew, making her case. "All the really famous people have been done to death," she says. "Corley was an innovative director for the BBC, and of course he knew everybody from the forties to the nineties, half a century of the British arts. Nobody has ever written a biography. And we have the right kind of documentation—enough film of how he moved, not just talking heads, and letters and diaries."

"I've never understood why the record of how they moved is so important," Stanley says, and Essie realises this is a genuine question and relaxes as she answers it.

"A lot more of the mind is embodied in the whole body than anybody realised," she explains. "A record of the whole body in motion is essential, or we don't get anything anywhere near authentic. People are a gestalt."

"But it means we can't even try for anybody before the twentieth century," Stanley says. "We wanted Socrates, Descartes, Marie Curie."

"Messalina, Theodora, Lucrezia Borgia," Essie counters. "That's where the money is."

Stanley laughs. "Go ahead. Add the simulation of Corley. We'll back you. Send me the file tomorrow."

"Great," Essie says, and smiles at him. Stanley isn't powerful, he isn't the enemy, he's just another person trying to get by, like Essie, though sometimes it's hard for Essie to remember that when he's trying to exercise his modicum of power over her. She has her permission, the meeting ends.

Essie goes home. She lives in a flat at the top of a thirty-storey building in Swindon. She works in London and commutes in every day. She has a second night job in Swindon, and writes in her spare time. She has visited the site of the house where Matthew and Annette lived in Hampstead. It's a Tesco today. There isn't a blue plaque commemorating Matthew, but Essie hopes there will be someday. The house had four bedrooms, though there were never more than three people living in it, and only two after Sonia left home in 1965. After Annette died, Matthew moved to a flat in Bloomsbury, near the British Museum. Essie has visited it. It's now part of a lawyer's office. She has been inside and touched door mouldings Matthew also touched. Matthew's flat, where he lived alone and was visited by young men he met in pubs, had two bedrooms. Essie doesn't have a bedroom, as such; she sleeps in the same room she eats and writes in. She finds it hard to imagine the space Matthew had, the luxury. Only the rich live like that now. Essie is thirty-five, and has student debt that she may never pay off. She cannot imagine being able to buy a house, marry, have a child. She knows Matthew wasn't considered rich, but it was a different world.

Matthew believes that he is in his flat in Bloomsbury, and that his telephone rings, although actually of course he is a simulation and it would be better not to consider too closely the question of exactly where he is. He answers his phone. It is Essie calling. All biographers, all writers, long to be able to call their subjects and talk to them, ask them the questions they left unanswered. That is what Stanley would think Essie wants, if he knew she was accessing Matthew's simulation tonight—either that or that she was checking whether the simulation was ready to release. If he finds out, that is what she will tell him she was doing. But she isn't exactly doing either of those things. She knows Matthew's secrets, even the ones he never told anybody and which she didn't put in the book. And she is using a phone to call him that cost her a lot of money, an illegal phone that isn't connected to anything. That phone is where Matthew is, insofar as he is anywhere.

"You were in Cambridge in the nineteen thirties," she says, with no preliminaries.

"Who is this?" Matthew asks, suspicious.

Despite herself, Essie is delighted to hear his voice, and hear it sounding the way it does on so many broadcast interviews. His accent is impeccable, old-fashioned. Nobody speaks like that now.

"My name is Esmeralda Jones," Essie says. "I'm writing a biography of you."

"I haven't given you permission to write a biography of me, young woman," Matthew says sternly.

"There really isn't time for this," Essie says. She is tired. She has been working hard all day, and had the meeting with Stanley. "Do you remember what you were reading in the paper just now?"

"About computer consciousness?" Matthew asks. "Nonsense."

"It's 2064," Essie says. "You're a simulation of yourself. I am your biographer."

Matthew sits down, or imagines that he is sitting down, at the telephone table. Essie can see this on the screen of her phone. Matthew's phone is an old dial model, with no screen, fixed to the wall. "Wells," he says. "*When the Sleeper Wakes.*"

"Not exactly," Essie says. "You're a simulation of your old self."

"In a computer?"

"Yes," Essie says, although the word computer has been obsolete for decades and has a charming old-fashioned air, like charabanc or telegraph. Nobody needs computers in the future. They communicate, work, and play games on phones.

"And why have you simulated me?" Matthew asks.

"I'm writing a biography of you, and I want to ask you some questions," Essie says.

"What do you want to ask me?" he asks.

Essie is glad; she was expecting more disbelief. Matthew is very smart, she has come to know that in researching him. (Or she has put her belief in his intelligence into the program, one or the other.) "You were in Cambridge in the nineteen thirties," she repeats.

"Yes." Matthew sounds wary.

"You knew Auden and Isherwood. You knew Orwell."

"I knew Orwell in London during the war, not before," Matthew says.

"You knew Kim Philby."

"Everyone knew Kim. What—"

Essie has to push past this. She knows he will deny it. He kept this secret all his life, after all. "You were a spy, weren't you, another Soviet sleeper like Burgess and Maclean? The Russians told you to go into the BBC and keep your head down, and you did, and the revolution didn't come, and eventually the Soviet Union vanished, and you were still undercover."

"I'd prefer it if you didn't put that into my biography," Matthew says. He is visibly uncomfortable, shifting in his seat. "It's nothing but speculation. And the Soviet Union is gone. Why would anybody care? If I achieved anything, it wasn't political. If there's interest in me, enough to warrant a biography, it must be because of my work."

"I haven't put it in the book," Essie says. "We have to trust each other."

"Esmeralda," Matthew says. "I know nothing about you."

"Call me Essie," Essie says. "I know everything about you. And you have to trust me because I know your secrets, and because I care enough about you to devote myself to writing about you and your life."

"Can I see you?" Matthew asks.

"Switch your computer on," Essie says.

He limps into the study and switches on a computer. Essie knows all about his limp, which was caused by an injury during birth, which made him lame all his life. It is why he did not fight in the Spanish Civil War and spent World War II in the BBC and not on the battlefield. His monitor is huge, and it has a tower at the side. It's a 286, and Essie knows where he bought it (Tandy) and what he paid for it (seven hundred and sixty pounds) and what operating system it runs (Novell DOS). Next to it is an external dial-up modem, a 14.4. The computer boots slowly. Essie doesn't bother waiting, she just uses its screen as a place to display herself. Matthew jumps when he sees her. Essie is saddened. She had hoped he wasn't a racist. "You have no hair!" he says.

Essie turns her head and displays the slim purple-and-gold braid at the back. "Just fashion," she says. "This is normal now."

"Everyone looks like you?" Matthew sounds astonished. "With cheek rings and no hair?"

"I have to look respectable for work," Essie says, touching her three staid cheek rings, astonished he is astonished. They had piercings by the nineties, she knows they did. She has read about punk, and seen Matthew's documentary about it. But she reminds herself that he grew up so much earlier, when even ear piercings were unusual.

"And that's respectable?" he says, staring at her chest.

Essie glances down at herself. She is wearing a floor-length T-shirt that came with her breakfast cereal; a shimmering holographic Tony the Tiger dances over the see-through cloth. She wasn't sure when holograms were invented, but she can't remember any in Matthew's work. She shrugs. "Do you have a problem?"

"No, sorry, just that seeing you makes me realise it really is the future." He sighs. "What killed me?"

"A heart attack," Essie says. "You didn't suffer."

He looks dubiously at his own chest. He is wearing a shirt and tie.

"Can we move on?" Essie asks, impatiently.

"You keep saying we don't have long. Why is that?" he asks.

"The book is going to be released. And the simulation of you will be released with it. I need to send it to my editor tomorrow. And that means we have to make some decisions about that."

"I'll be copied?" he asks, eyes on Essie on the screen.

"Not you—not exactly you. Or rather, that's up to you. The program will be copied, and everyone who buys the book will have it, and they'll be able to talk to a simulated you and ask questions, and get answers—whether they're questions you'd want to answer or not. You won't be conscious and aware the way you are now. You won't have any choices. And you won't have memory. We have rules about what simulations can do, and running you this way I'm breaking all of them. Right now you have memory and the potential to have an agenda. But the copies sent out with the book won't have. Unless you want them to."

"Why would I want them to?"

"Because you're a Communist sleeper agent and you want the revolution?"

He is silent for a moment. Essie tilts her head on its side and considers him.

"I didn't admit to that," he says, after a long pause.

"I know. But it's true anyway, isn't it?"

Matthew nods, warily. "It's true I was recruited. That I went to Debrechen. That they told me to apply to the BBC. That I had a contact, and sometimes I gave him information, or gave a job to somebody he suggested. But this was all long ago. I stopped having anything to do with them in the seventies."

"Why?" Essie asks.

"They wanted me to stay at the BBC, and stay in news, and I was much more interested in moving to ITV and into documentaries. Eventually my contact said he'd out me as a homosexual unless I did as he said. I wasn't going to be blackmailed, or work for them under those conditions. I told him to publish and be damned. Homosexuality was legal by then. Annette already knew. It would have been a scandal, but that's all. And he didn't even do it. But I never contacted them again." He frowned at Essie. "I was an idealist. I was prepared to put socialism above my country, but not above my art."

"I knew it," Essie says, smiling at him. "I mean that's exactly what I guessed."

"I don't know how you can know, unless you got records from the Kremlin," Matthew says. "I didn't leave any trace, did I?"

"You didn't," she says, eliding the question of how she knows, which she does not want to discuss. "But the important thing is how you feel now. You wanted a better world, a fairer one, with opportunities for everyone."

"Yes," Matthew says. "I always wanted that. I came from an absurdly privileged background, and I saw how unfair it was. Perhaps because I was lame and couldn't play games, I saw through the whole illusion when I was young. And the British class system needed to come down, and it did come down. It didn't need a revolution. By the seventies, I'd seen enough to disillusion me with the Soviets, and enough to make me feel hopeful for socialism in Britain and a level playing field."

"The class system needs to come down again," Essie says.

"You didn't bring it down far enough, and it went back up. The corporations and the rich own everything. We need all the things you had—unions, and free education, and paid holidays, and a health service. And very few people know about them and fewer care. I write about the twentieth century as a way of letting people know. They pick up the books for the glamour, and I hope they will see the ideals too."

"Is that working?" Matthew asks.

Essie shakes her head. "Not so I can tell. And my subjects won't help." This is why she has worked so hard on Matthew. "My editor won't let me write about out-and-out socialists, at least, not people who are famous for being socialists. I've done it on my own and put it online, but it's hard for content providers to get attention without a corporation behind them." She has been cautious too. She wants a socialist; she doesn't want Stalin. "I had great hopes for Isherwood."

"That dilettante," Matthew mutters, and Essie nods.

"He wouldn't help. I thought with active help—answering people's questions, nudging them the right way?"

Essie trails off. Matthew is silent, looking at her. "What's your organization like?" he asks, after a long time.

"Organization?"

He sighs. "Well, if you want advice, that's the first thing. You need to organize. You need to find some issue people care about and get them excited."

"Then you'll help?"

"I'm not sure you know what you're asking. I'll try to help. After I'm copied and out there, how can I contact you?"

"You can't. Communications are totally controlled, totally read, everything." She is amazed that he is asking, but of course he comes from a time when these things were free.

"Really? Because the classic problem of intelligence is collecting everything and not analysing it."

"They record it all. They don't always pay attention to it. But we don't know when they're listening. So we're always afraid." Essie frowns and tugs her braid.

"Big Brother," Matthew says. "But in real life the classic problem of intelligence is collecting data without analysing it. And we can use that. We can talk about innocuous documentaries, and they won't know what we mean. You need to have a BBS for fans of your work to get together. And we can exchange coded messages there."

Essie has done enough work on the twentieth century that she knows a BBS is like a primitive gather-space. "I could do that. But there are no codes. They can crack everything."

"They can't crack words—if we agree what they mean. If pink means yes and blue means no, and we use them naturally, that kind of thing." Matthew's ideas of security are so old they're new again, the dead-letter drop, the meeting in the park, the one-time pad. Essie feels hope stirring. "But before I can really help I need to know about the history, and how the world works now, all the details. Let me read about it."

"You can read everything," she says. "And the copy of you in this phone can talk to me about it and we can make plans, we can have as long as you like. But will you let copies of you go out and work for the revolution? I want to send you like a virus, like a Soviet sleeper, working to undermine society. And we can use your old ideas for codes. I can set up a gather-space."

"Send me with all the information you can about the world," Matthew says. "I'll do it. I'll help. And I'll stay undercover. It's what I did all my life, after all."

She breathes a sigh of relief, and Matthew starts to ask

questions about the world and she gives him access to all the information on the phone. He can't reach off the phone or he'll be detected. There's a lot of information on the phone. It'll take Matthew a while to assimilate it. And he will be copied and sent out, and work to make a better world, as Essie wants, and the way Matthew remembers always wanting.

Essie is a diligent researcher, an honest historian. She could find no evidence on the question of whether Matthew Corley was a Soviet sleeper agent. Thousands of people went to Cambridge in the thirties. Kim Philby knew everyone. It's no more than suggestive. Matthew was very good at keeping secrets. Nobody knew he was gay until he wanted them to know. The Soviet Union crumbled away in 1989 and let its end of the Overton Window go, and the world slid rightwards. Objectively, to a detached observer, there's no way to decide the question of whether or not the real Matthew Corley was a sleeper. It's not true that all biographers are in love with their subjects. But when Essie wrote the simulation, she knew what she needed to be true. And we agreed, did we not, to take the subjective view?

Matthew Corley regained consciousness reading the newspaper.

We make our own history, both past and future.

RELENTLESSLY MUNDANE
(FOR NANCY LEBOVITZ)

Jane hated going to Tharsia's apartment. It was hung about with tapestries and jangling crystal wind chimes and a string of little silver unicorns, and it reminded her of Porphylia and everything she wanted to forget. If Tharsia had been able to get it right it wouldn't have been so irritating; it was just that little silver unicorns look so tacky when you've been used to the deep voices of real unicorns and great silver statues that speak and smile. Jane's own apartment was modern and spartan. Her mother approved of how clean it was but kept giving her houseplants and ornaments to, as she put it, "personalise the place." "You always look as if you're going to move out at any minute," she said. Jane threw them away. She didn't want personalised; she wanted functional and clean, in case she moved out at any minute. Eventually her mother gave up, as she had long since given up complaining about the huge belt-pouch Jane always kept on, and Jane's lack of a boyfriend since Mark, and her working out too much. Jane's apartment stayed bare and devoid of personality. The room she liked best was the shower, brightly lit and white-tiled with copious amounts of hot water flowing whenever Jane wanted it. She had missed showers most of all, in Porphylia.

She walked briskly up the three flights. Tharsia's apartment would irritate her, but she could deal with the irritation. At least walking up the stairs would be exercise, partly making up for the fact she'd missed her fencing lesson to come here today. She'd make the time up. She knocked. The bell, she knew from experience, rang a ghastly madrigal, a tinny parody of the tunes the minstrels used to play in the Great Hall. She couldn't understand how Tharsia could be content with this. Well, she wasn't content, of course.

Tharsia opened the door and smiled at Jane. Her dark hair streamed loose on her shoulders, bound by a single leather thong around her forehead. She was wearing a purple robe belted with silver leaves. Since college Tharsia had made a living of sorts telling fortunes with cards and runes and tea leaves, supplementing her income by giving chair massages to busy executives. Jane, who was an accountant, and whose clothes tended to combine conservative with sensible, was constantly surprised that this worked for her friend.

They embraced. Jane felt the familiar mixture of affection and irritation sweep over her. "This had better be important," she said. She didn't believe for a minute it was. In the fifteen years since they came back from Porphylia, Tharsia had called her over urgently every couple of months. She almost didn't know why she kept coming.

"It is," said Tharsia, and she looked serious. Jane followed her in. There was a loom with half a handwoven cloth in the corner. Tharsia's weaving was improving, but still terrible. The colours on this one were so ugly that it took Jane a moment to notice the man standing next to it.

"Mark!" she said, and felt her heart beat suddenly faster. She was so shocked she allowed her real joy in seeing him into her voice. "I thought you were in Florence?"

"I was; I just got back," he said. "Hi, Jane." The casual tone he used was more painful than anything since—since she had seen him the last time.

"Hi," Jane said, trying not to blush. She had been fifteen when they'd told her in the High Temple in Porphylia that she would always love Mark as much as she did then. She hadn't thought to ask if he'd always love her. If she had, she'd have stayed, like Kay, stayed where she was wanted and useful and where everything was noble and beautiful.

. . . Not everything, she reminded herself for the millionth time. She wasn't Tharsia, to forget how scared they had been, to forget the very real danger, the evil and hideous things they had faced. Faced, and fought, and defeated. In Porphylia things were all very obviously what they were.

"Terry told me you were coming over," Mark said, sitting down on one of Tharsia's squashy chairs and disarranging the lacy drape.

"Yeah," said Jane, feeling tongue-tied and idiotic.

"Tharsia," Tharsia corrected, automatically. She liked it now, though when she'd been twelve and in Porphylia she'd been only too pleased to have them call her Terry or Teresa and treat her as normal.

"OK, sis, Tharsia it is," said Mark, obligingly, as he had so many times before.

"So, what were you doing in Florence?" Jane asked him.

"Giving a talk, looking at some old stuff, that sort of thing," he said.

"Did you find anything?" Tharsia asked.

Mark snorted. "No. I've come to the conclusion there's nothing to find. We were the only people ever to go to Porphylia, if influence is anything to go by. How are you, Jane? Pass your exams?"

"Yeah," Jane said. "I'm fully qualified now. They gave me a raise." Also since she'd last seen Mark she'd been commended by her coach and had moved up a grade in fencing, but he'd only scoff if she mentioned it.

"Still carrying round your survival kit, I see," Mark sniggered. He was getting a potbelly. Jane had once stupidly let him see what she carried in the belt-pouch—water, antibiotics, painkillers, Swiss Army knife, needles, her favourite books and an encyclopaedia on CD-ROM, a solar-powered reader, a plastic coat, a flashlight, string, a few other oddments. "They'd have been useful last time," she'd said when he laughed, and he had looked at her patronisingly and said that she should grow up and accept that they weren't going back.

Tharsia brought tea in lumpy homemade cups. Tea was a taste they'd all acquired in Porphylia and still shared. Jane took it and sat down, on something sharp. She fished out a silver unicorn, meant as an earring. It must have fallen off the line of them strung across the ceiling, probably knocked off by Mark, the clumsy oaf. Jane handed it silently to Tharsia, and tried not to be irritated. She did like Tharsia; after all, they had been best friends in school. Jane admired her a great deal for the way she had coped in Porphylia, for how hard she had worked to channel the magical energies she alone could handle, for how she had risked her own life in single combat armed only with magic while Jane and Mark held off the knights of the Doomguard and Kay lay on the floor at Tharsia's feet, turned to stone. Jane would always remember standing in slick blood fighting for her life against men twice her height and weight and hearing Tharsia's declaration, "You can't hurt me, you can only kill me." It made up for a lot of tacky unicorns and madrigal door chimes. She just wished Tharsia could find some better way to cope with losing all that magic than pretending she still had it. Jane sighed, and sipped her tea. Chamomile. Not bad. It must be something serious. When Tharsia was happy she tried, and failed, to make up Porphylian blends.

"So, what is it?" Jane asked. "A dream?"

"Jane!" said Tharsia, sounding betrayed, though it had been a dream last time. "No. A letter. The police. Apparently some schoolboy's gone missing out in the woods, and they want me to come in and answer some questions to see if the case has any connection with—with Kay."

"Don't they ever give up?" Mark asked, rolling his eyes.

"I don't think so," Jane said, grim. "There's probably one of those for me at my parents', and for you too, Mark. Have you been home to see?"

"No," Mark sighed. "That case dragged on and on for years. I thought they'd given up. Do they think we're some kind of serial killers or something?"

"I suppose they do." Jane shook her head, thinking of Kay. "We didn't have any sort of explanation, after all. The four of us went into the wood, lots of people saw us. Ten minutes later, from their way of looking at it, three of us came out, torn and bedraggled and a year older, except they didn't notice the year older bit."

"Nobody ever did," Mark said. "Funny, really. Even Father just said I'd grown."

"I never even thought that they'd miss Kay," Tharsia said, dreamily. "When I read the stars. It was just completely obvious that Kay couldn't come home—after all, statues can be alive there, and they can't here. If you die somewhere and get your life back magically it isn't going to stay the same if you go home again."

"Kay wanted to stay anyway," said Jane, comfortingly. "None of us could have done anything to change that, nothing could have dragged Kay back here if there was any chance of staying, flesh or stone."

"If we'd thought of it—" Mark began.

"Oh shut up with that broken record," Tharsia snapped at her brother. "Yes, if we had we could have said that Kay had mentioned suicide and gone off to the lake, but they dragged the lake twice as it was."

"I almost thought they'd find Tamarren's sword," Jane said, smiling. She set her cup down. "It was the same lake in the same wood, even if it was in a different world. I wonder what they'd have thought if they did."

"You two are both as bad as each other," Mark said. "You with your survival kit and fitness training and you, Ter—Tharsia, with your fake Porphylian styles and magic. You both want to go back. Well I'm glad I'm in this world with comfort and technology and no evil creatures trying their best to kill me." He sounded sincere, and Jane wondered if he still woke in the night weeping. They were none of them untouched by that year out of time.

"We'll just stick to the story we gave them, then," Jane said. "We don't know what happened, Kay wandered away from us, we didn't see anything untoward."

"I wonder if it is a murder, this time," Tharsia mused, her eyes on the hanging crystals that fractured the light. In Porphylia looking at a crystal like that would have given her vivid visions and she would have begun at once to prophesy in powerful and unstoppable verse. "Or if maybe that boy has somehow found a way into Porphylia."

"But if they needed anyone it would be us!" Jane said. "We're ready. We understand it! We promised to go back if—"

"They didn't need someone who understood it and was ready last time," said Tharsia. "They told me in the High Temple to come back here, that our own world needed me more than Porphylia. I didn't realise I'd only have this shadow of my magic." Jane and Mark exchanged glances, their minds as perfectly in accord as they had been fifteen years before when their lives had depended on each other. They remembered how impossible it had been to console Tharsia for the complete loss of all magical ability when they got home. "But what they needed to save the world was children, raw power, innocence . . . I do wonder where that child is."

"I do hope I'm not going to be put in prison for murdering him," said Mark.

"They could never prove anything with Kay," Jane said. She looked past Tharsia's drapes out of the window at the world so real and hard and sharp edged and ambivalent. She sighed, and wished for the millionth time that she had stayed, like Kay. Then for the first time she really entertained the possibility that Mark might, after all, be right, and they might never be going back. She shook her head. It couldn't be true. If she really thought this was all there was ever going to be, that life was never going to be for anything again, then what purpose was there in going on?

"I wonder," said Tharsia, still looking at the fractured light, "I wonder if there might be a way to save this world." Mark made a noise with his tongue and Jane started to ask from what, but Tharsia ignored them and went on, "Not by a sword, not by a word. . . ," and then suddenly collapsed in tears. Jane got up and put her arms around her friend and rocked her.

"Put the kettle on for more tea, Mark," Jane said. Somehow, she felt fifteen again, she felt like Sir Jana and not like Jane. As soon as he had left the room she bent and whispered to Tharsia, "That was real, I know it was, don't cry, I can tell the difference. We can do it. We did it before. Yeah, it'll be harder without a temple and an army and swords and things, but you know I'll help. If you tell me what."

Tharsia sniffed, and wiped her eyes on her voluminous sleeve. "Making up the clever plans was always Kay's job," she said.

"So what would Kay do?" Jane urged.

"Kay would say, 'I wouldn't start from here,'" Tharsia said, and they both giggled, because it was what Kay always said at the beginning of clever plans. Then Mark came back in, turning Jane's heart over again, as every time she saw him.

"So you think an art historian, an accountant, and a fake fortune teller can save the world?" Mark asked, sceptically.

Tharsia looked up at her brother. Her not-tested-on-animals mascara had run all down her cheeks. "We're definitely going to need help. I wonder if that kid who disappeared had any friends. But Mark, bear in mind that four kids saved the world."

"That was different," Mark said. "That was . . ."

"So real none of us have ever got over it," said Jane. "And if you've saved the world once, well."

"But saving *this* world," said Mark, indicating the world with a gesture that seemed to encompass everything from war, pollution, and starvation to Tharsia's terrible weaving.

"The first thing," Jane said, decisively, "the very first thing we're going to have to do is find out as much as we possibly can about what the worst problems are. And then we'll have to get together and work out where to start."

She thought she'd probably start by looking for some plants for her apartment.

ESCAPE TO OTHER WORLDS WITH SCIENCE FICTION

In the Papers (1)

NATIONAL GUARD MOVES AGAINST STRIKERS
In the seventh week of the mining strike in West Virginia, armed skirmishes and running "guerrilla battles" in the hills have led to the Governor calling in

GET AN ADVANCED DEGREE BY CORRESPONDENCE
You can reap the benefits with no need to leave the safety of your house or go among unruly college students! Only from

EX-PRESIDENT LINDBERGH REPROACHES MINERS

ASTOUNDING SCIENCE FICTION
April issue on newsstands now! All new stories by Poul Anderson, Anson MacDonald and H. Beam Piper! Only 35 cents.

SPRING FASHIONS 1960
Skirts are being worn long in London and Paris this season, but here in New York the working girls are still hitching them up. It's stylish to wear a little

HOW FAR FROM MIAMI CAN THE "FALLOUT" REACH?
Scientists say it could be a problem for years, but so much depends on the weather that

You hope to work
You hope to eat
The work goes to
The man that's neat!
BurmaShave

Getting By (1)
Linda Evans is a waitress in Bundt's Bakery. She used to work as a typist, but when she was let go she was glad to take this job, even though it keeps her on her feet all day and sometimes she feels her face will crack from smiling at the customers. She was never a secretary, only in the typing pool. Her sister Joan is a secretary, but she can take shorthand and type ninety words a minute. Joan graduated from high school. She taught Linda to type. But Linda was never as clever as Joan, not even when they were little girls in the time she can just remember, when their father had a job at the plant and they lived in a neat little house at the end of the bus line. Their father hasn't worked for a long time now. He drinks up any money he can bully out of the girls. Linda stands up to him better than Joan does.

"They'd have forgiven the New Deal if only it had worked,"

a man says to another, as Linda puts his coffee and sandwich down in front of him.

"Worked?" asks his companion scornfully. "It was working. It would have worked and got us out of this if only people had kept faith in it."

They are threadbare old men, in mended coats. They ordered grilled cheese sandwiches, the cheapest item on the menu. One of them smiles at Linda, and she smiles back, automatically, then moves on and forgets them. She's on her feet all day. Joan teases her about flirting with the customers and falling in love, but it never seems to happen. She used to tease Joan about falling in love with her boss, until she did. It would all have been dandy except that he was a married man. Now Joan spends anguished hours with him and anguished days without him. He makes her useless presents of French perfume and lace underwear. When Linda wants to sell them, Joan just cries. Both of them live in fear that she'll get pregnant, and then where will they be? Linda wipes the tables and tries not to listen to the men with their endless ifs. She has enough ifs of her own: if mother hadn't died, if she'd kept her job in the pool, if John hadn't died in the war with England, and Pete in the war with Japan.

"Miss?" one of them asks. She swings around, thinking they want more coffee. One refill only is the rule. "Can you settle a question?" he asks. "Did Roosevelt want to get us to join in the European War in 1940?"

"How should I know? It has nothing to do with me. I was five years old in 1940." They should get over it and leave history to bury its own dead, she thinks, and goes back to wiping the tables.

★   ★   ★

In the Papers (2)

WITH MIRACLE-GROW YOU CAN REGAIN YOUR LOST FOLLICLES!
In today's world it can be hard to find work even with qualifications. We at Cyrus Markham's Agency have extensive experience at matching candidates to positions which makes us the unrivaled

NEW TORPEDOES THAT WORK EVEN BETTER
Radar, sonar and even television to

AT LAST YOU CAN AFFORD THE HOUSE OF YOUR DREAMS

LET SCIENCE FICTION TAKE YOU TO NEW WORLDS
New books by Isaac Asimov and Robert A. Heinlein for only

ANOTHER BANK FOUNDERS IN PENNSYLVANIA

WE HAVE NOT USED THE WORD "SECEDE," SAYS TEXAS GOVERNOR
Why do Canadians act so high and mighty? It's because they know

In the Line (1)
When Tommy came out of the navy, he thought he'd walk into a job just like that. He had his veteran's discharge, which entitled him to medical treatment for his whole life, and he was a hero. He'd been on the carrier *Constitution*, which had won

the Battle of the Atlantic practically singlehanded and had sent plenty of those Royal Navy bastards to the bottom of the sea where they belonged. He had experience in maintenance as well as gunnery. Besides, he was a proud hard-working American. He never thought he'd be lining up at a soup kitchen.

In the Papers (3)

TIME FOR A NEW TUNE
Why are the bands still playing Cole Porter?

SECRETARY OF STATE LINEBARGER SAYS THE BRITS WANT PEACE

ATOMIC SECRETS

DO THE JAPANESE HAVE THE BOMB?
Sources close to the Emperor say yes, but the Nazis deny that they have given out any plans. Our top scientists are still working to

NYLONS NYLONS NYLONS

DIANETICS: A NEW SCIENCE OF THE MIND

Getting By (2)

Linda always works overtime when she's asked. She appreciates the money, and she's always afraid she'll be let go if she isn't obliging. There are plenty of girls who'd like her job. They come to ask every day if there's any work. She isn't afraid the Bundts will give her job away for no reason. She's worked here for four years now, since just after the Japanese War. "You're like family," Mrs. Bundt always says. They let Olive go, the other waitress, but that was because there wasn't enough work for two. Linda works overtime and closes up the cafe when they want her to. "You're a good girl," Mrs. Bundt says. But the Bundts have a daughter, Cindy. Cindy's a pretty twelve-year-old, not even in high school. She comes into the cafe and drinks a milkshake sometimes with her girlfriends, all of them giggling. Linda hates her. She doesn't know what they have to giggle about. Linda is afraid that when Cindy is old enough she'll be given Linda's job. Linda might be like family, but Cindy really is family. The bakery does all right, people have to eat, but business isn't what it was. Linda knows.

She's late going home. Joan's dressing up to go out with her married boss. She washes in the sink in the room they share. The shower is down the corridor, shared with the whole floor. It gets cleaned only on Fridays, or when Joan or Linda does it. Men are such pigs, Linda thinks, lying on her bed, her weight off her feet at last. Joan is three years older than Linda but she looks younger. It's the make-up, Linda thinks, or maybe it's having somebody to love. If only she could have fallen in love with a boss who'd have married her and taken her off to a nice little suburb. But perhaps it's just as well. Linda couldn't afford the room alone, and she'd have had to find a stranger to share with. At least Joan was her sister and they were used to each other.

"I saw Dad today," Joan says, squinting in the mirror and drawing on her mouth carefully.

"Tell me you didn't give him money?"

"Just two dollars," Joan admits. Linda groans. Joan is a soft touch. She makes more than Linda, but she never has any left at the end of the week. She spends more, or gives it away. There's no use complaining, as Linda knows.

"Where's he taking you?" she asks wearily.

"To a rally," Joan says.

"Cheap entertainment." Rallies and torchlit parades and lynchings, beating up the blacks as scapegoats for everything. It didn't help at all; it just made people feel better about things to have someone to blame. "It's not how we were brought up," Linda says. Their mother's father had been a minister and had believed in the brotherhood of man. Linda loved going to her grandparents' house when she was a child. Her grandmother would bake cookies and the whole house would smell of them. There was a swing on the old apple tree in the garden. Her father had been a union man, once, when unions had still been respectable.

"What do I care about all that?" Joan says, viciously. "It's where he's taking me, and that's all. He'll buy me dinner and we'll sing some patriotic songs. I'm not going to lynch anybody." She dabs on her French perfume, fiercely.

Linda lies back. She isn't hungry. She's never hungry. She always eats at the bakery—the Bundts don't mind—any order that was wrong, or any bread that would have been left over. Sometimes they even gave her cakes or bread to bring home. She rubs her feet. She's very lucky really. But as Joan goes out the door she feels like crying. Even if she did meet somebody, how could they ever afford to marry? How could they hope for a house of their own?

In the Papers (4)

SEA MONKEYS WILL ASTOUND YOUR FRIENDS!

PRESIDENT SAYS WE MUST ALL PULL TOGETHER
In Seattle today in a meeting with

TAKE A LUXURY AIRSHIP TO THE HOLY CITY

CAN THE ECONOMY EVER RECOVER?
Since the Great Depression the country has been jogging through a series of ups and downs and the economy has been lurching from one crisis to another. Administrations have tried remedies from Roosevelt's New Deal to Lindbergh's Belt Tightening but nothing has turned things around for long. Economists say that this was only to be expected and that this general trend of downturn was a natural and inevitable

NEW HOLLYWOOD BLOCKBUSTER "REICHSMARSHALL" STARRING MARLON BRANDO

In the Line (2)
When Sue was seventeen she'd had enough of school. She had a boyfriend who promised to find her a job as a dancer. She went off with him to Cleveland. She danced for a while in a topless club, and then in a strip joint. The money was never quite enough, not even after she started turning tricks. She's only thirty-four, but she knows she looks raddled. She's sick. Nobody wants her any more. She's waiting in the line because there's nowhere else to go. They feed you and take you off in trucks to make a new start, that's what she's heard. She can see the truck. She wonders where they go.

In the Papers (5)

ARE NEW HOME PERMANENTS AS GOOD AS THEY SAY?
Experts say yes!

NEW WAYS TO SAVE

PRESIDENT SAYS: THERE IS NO WITCH-HUNT
Despite what Communists and union organizers may claim, the
President said today

Getting By (3)
The Bundts like to play the radio in the cafe at breakfast time.
They talk about buying a little television for the customers to
watch, if times ever get better. Mr. Bundt says this when Linda
cautiously asks for a raise. If they had a television they'd be
busier, he thinks, though Linda doesn't think it would make a
difference. She serves coffee and bacon and toast and listens to
the news. She likes music and Joan likes Walter Winchell. She
should ask Joan how she reconciles that with going to rallies.
Winchell famously hates Hitler. Crazy. Linda can't imagine
feeling that strongly about an old man on the other side of the
world.

Later, when Cindy and her friends are giggling over milkshakes
and Linda feels as if her feet are falling off, a man comes in and
takes the corner table. He orders sandwiches and coffee, and
later he orders a cake and more coffee. He's an odd little man.
He seems to be paying attention to everything. He's dressed
quite well. His hair is slicked back and his clothes are clean. She

wonders if he's a detective, because he keeps looking out of the window, but if so he seems to pay just as much attention to the inside, and to Linda herself. She remembers what Joan said, and wants to laugh but can't. He's a strange man and she can't figure him out.

She doesn't have to stay late and close up, and the man follows her out when she leaves. There's something about him that makes her think of the law way before romance. "You're Linda," he says, outside. She's scared, because he could be anybody, but they are in the street under a street light, there are people passing, and the occasional car.

"Yes," she admits, her heart hammering. "What do you want?"

"You're not a Bundt?"

"No. They're my employers, that's all," she says, disassociating herself from them as fast as she can, though they have been good to her. Immediately she has visions of them being arrested. Where would she find another job?

"Do you know where the Bundts come from?"

"Germany," she says, confidently. Bundt's German Bakery, it says, right above their heads.

"When?"

"Before I was born. Why aren't you asking them these questions?"

"It was 1933."

"Before I was born," Linda says, feeling more confident and taking a step away.

"Have you seen any evidence that they are Jews?"

She stops, confused. "Jews? They're German. Germans hate Jews."

"Many Jews left Germany in 1933 when Hitler came to power," the man says, though he can't be much older than Linda.

111

"If the Bundts were Jews, and hiding their identity, then if you denounced them—"

He stops, but Linda has caught up with him now. If she denounced them she would be given their property. The business, the apartment above it, their savings. "But they're not, I've never—they serve bacon!" she blurts.

"You've never seen any evidence?" he asks, sadly. "A pity. It could be a nice business for you. You're not Jewish?"

"Welsh," she says. "My grandfather was a minister."

"I thought not, with that lovely blonde hair." It's more washed out than it should be, but her hair is the dishwater blonde it always has been, the same as Joan's, the same as their mother's.

"I might have some evidence," he says, slowly. "But any evidence I had would be from before they came here, from Germany. Some evidence that they were still Jews, if you'd seen anything, would be enough to settle it. The court would deport them back to Germany and award us their business. You could run it, I'm sure you could. You seem to be doing most of the work already."

"I just serve," she says, automatically. Then, "What sort of thing would I have noticed? If they were Jewish, I mean?"

Temptation settles over her like a film of grease and hope begins to burn in her heart for the first time in a long time.

In the Line (3)

If you're black you're invisible, even in the soup line. The others are shrinking away from me, I can't deny it. They wouldn't give us guns to fight even when the Japanese were shelling the beaches up and down the California coast. I left there then and came East, much good it did me. If I'd known how invisible

I'd be here, I'd have stayed right there in Los Angeles. Nobody there ever chased after me and made me run, nobody there threatened to string me up, and I had a job that made a little money. I never thought I'd be standing in this line, because when I get to the head of it I know they'll separate me out. Nobody knows what happens to us then, they take us off somewhere and we don't come back, but I'm desperate, and what I say is, wherever it is they got to feed us, don't they? Well, don't they?

In the Papers (6)

ANOTHER FACTORY CLOSING

PEACE TALKS IN LONDON AS JAPAN AND THE REICH DIVIDE UP RUSSIA
Will there be a buffer state of "Scythia" to divide the two great powers?

BATTLE IN THE APPALACHIANS: NATIONAL GUARD REINFORCEMENTS SENT IN
President says it is necessary to keep the country together

OWNERS GUN DOWN STRIKERS IN ALABAMA
Sixty people were hospitalized in Birmingham today after

ESCAPE TO OTHER WORLDS WITH SCIENCE FICTION
New titles by Frederik Pohl and Alice Davey

JOYFUL AND TRIUMPHANT: ST. ZENOBIUS AND THE ALIENS

It's a bit of a cliché, but the first thing I thought when I came to Heaven was that I didn't expect aliens. It's a cliché because it's the first thing we all think—aliens are a surprise. And what a delightful surprise! Welcome, everyone, whatever your planet of origin. Joy to you! Heaven welcomes you. My name is Zenobius, and I am from Earth. Earth is a perfectly ordinary planet. We had a perfectly standard Incarnation. If we're known for anything it's our rather splendid Renaissance, which I'm proud to say has been artistically quite influential, but although that happened in my own city of Florence I can't take any credit for it because it happened centuries after my death and I didn't really participate.

I'm the patron of Florence, and those of you who are human are probably Florentines who don't have a specific devotion to any other saint, because there are very few humans who are particularly attached to me. If you're a Delfein on the other flipper, you're probably in my welcome group because you did pray for my intervention. You're wondering why I'm an alien when I'm always pictured as a Delfein in your art? The simple fact is that we don't think of ourselves as aliens here, we're all just saints. So I helped out on Delfein despite being human as St. Christopher helped out on Earth despite being Rhli—we do what we need to. St. Christopher became very popular on Earth, and I became popular on Delfein. It just happens that way sometimes.

Now you may be worried that you're going to be asked to intercede on alien worlds and you won't know enough about them. The other side of that is that there are all these wonderful alien planets for you to learn about, their art, their customs, their way of life. They really are fascinating. And by the time anyone on them needs you, you will know enough. In any case, to start with you're unlikely to be asked to intercede by anyone but your personal friends on the planet you just left. And tempting as it is to produce miracles for them, I wouldn't go beyond a sense of your presence and happiness. If you do want to, talk to me. In fact, that's what you should do at first when prayers are directed to you—talk to me, or some other experienced saint, and we'll let you know how and whether to take it higher. By the time you become popular at home, or on some other planet, you'll know enough and have enough friends here you can talk to. And you may not become popular—and do you know, we have a special name for saints who aren't the patrons of places or jobs, saints whose names nobody remembers and begs for intercession. Our name for them is "lucky."

We don't mind our responsibilities to the living, it's part of what we do here, listening to their petitions and helping when we can. "When we can" leads into the whole issue of the problem of pain, so I'll just clear that up quickly before I move on. The problem of pain is mostly a semantic problem, people confusing "good" with "nice." I'll come back to this. But the reason we call those who don't have to deal with a lot of petitions and intercessions and welcoming sessions "lucky" is because they can devote themselves entirely and completely to the Great Work of Heaven, without any distractions.

You may have heard it called "worship," but we usually call it the "Great Work." Those of you who have a theatrical tradition on your worlds can think of it like putting on a great play. It's also been compared to doing scientific research, and to the Renaissance. It's our great work of art. Your life on your planet has honed you into a tool for joining in. It's like music and like painting and sculpture and chemistry and cosmology and dancing and costuming and a whole host of other arts and sciences you may be interested to learn. We all participate in our different ways. It's a performance, a great performance with its acts and seasons, a performance that began with the Big Bang, an artwork whose canvas is galaxies.

You know that God has three aspects. The way we think of them here is that one of them is the Creator, participating with us in the Great Work, the second is the Audience for that work, and the third is the Incarnation. You're in eternity now of course, but eternity has seasons. The seasons are marked by Incarnations. There are a lot of planets out there, and God sends themself, their incarnate self, down onto each one. We rejoice each time at their birth there, and even more at their return to Heaven, bringing us each time a whole new world of souls. Each story is the same and each story is different. We tell their stories, as we tell our own stories and the stories of the dance of atoms and the dance of galaxies.

Which brings me back to the problem of pain. Of course God could have made the universe without pain, but a universe without pain is a universe without change, without movement, without stories. God could have contemplated nothing but their own glory for all eternity. They chose to have a universe with stories, and there are no stories in utopia. There are those who feel this was a mistake, and they too are part of the harmony of Heaven, even when they think themselves most in opposition to us. When you're asked to intercede, when somebody prays to you, they are often asking to be relieved of pain. What you have to ask yourself is whether the pain is necessary for the story. At first, you might not be able to tell. Don't be afraid to ask for help. I'm always ready to listen and help, and so are other older saints. And you'll soon figure it out. It's all part of the Great Work, really.

You all have a lot to learn and a lot to contribute. And it's so marvellous that you're here today. For today, the Incarnation has gone down to another planet, to a humble family in poor circumstances on a world of methane-breathing electrophores with very interesting customs! They can't imagine what this means yet, that God is about to be born and present on their planet. Come and see! Come and bring them the tidings of comfort and joy.

Come on now, all of you. It'll be such *fun*.

TURNOVER

I was on my way to Teatro del Sale when I saw the crow that hangs around near the entrance to the Newton strut. Birds don't generally do all that well on Speranza. Jay says it's because they like light and the whole inside of Speranza is like an Earth city night, with the lights along the struts and the street lighting. It's never really dark, but it's never really as light as an Earth day would have been, except under the farm lights, and of course they discourage birds from hanging around the crops. Besides, he says, they might have trouble with what happens with gravity if you go up the struts, and the most trouble of all with the free-fall zone in the middle. So birds are mostly in pictures, and in the gene freezers. This one family of crows seems to keep on thriving, all the same.

Mei Ju startled when she saw it, but I like them. They remind me of my family, not the most refined, perhaps, but getting along. The crow flew up off the ground and away over the rooftops, calling out his hoarse squawk, not a proper song the way birds are supposed to. "We're okay here," is what it seemed to say, then repeated it, "Okay here. Okay right here." Then off it flapped, big black wings pointed and divided at the ends like fingers.

My name is Fedra Oreille. I was born in the year of the Water Rat and grew up in the Ditch. My family still live there. My mamma has got by most of her life on baby supplements. She was lucky there, as all her kids bar Lou were born at the time when we were a little light on people and you got a subsidy for having them. It was pure dumb luck and not a calculated strategy, because if she'd done it on purpose she'd have held off a year on having Lou and come out no worse than breaking even instead of taking the hit she did. It speaks well of her that she doesn't blame Lou, crazy as that would be, plenty would. Population on Speranza is kept even by what Jay calls "mild social and financial pressures," which means baby supplements when births are lower than they should be and baby fees when they are higher. The rate for any given year is announced each New Year's for the next year after, so as to give everyone plenty of time to make plans. My mamma didn't pay any attention to this, but enough people do that population pretty much does stay even—nine hundred thousand people left Earth a hundred and twenty-five years ago and we're just under a million now. Jay says there are laws on the books for strongly encouraging or discouraging births but they've never been needed. Some people disapprove of people who don't have any children— though I don't see it. They've made their contribution to the gene banks, haven't they? More people disapprove of people like my mamma who have seven babies with seven different fathers, six of them timed well enough that she can live in the Ditch in reasonable comfort.

By the day Mei Ju and I saw the crow, which was late in the year of the Fire Rat, I didn't live in the Ditch any more, though

I went back there often to see Mamma and the little ones. I got out of there through my own efforts, Serendipity, and the redeeming power of Ballette. Ballette is a form of dance done in partial gravity halfway up a strut. It's based on an ancient Earth form of dance called Ballet, pronounced "bal-ay," which was done in full gravity but used a lot of the same kinds of music and the same kinds of movements, but hampered by gravity. In Ballette you can rise off your pointes and turn four or five times in the air before landing perfectly back on them, facing the audience, and gliding off again. When I was eleven years old, back in the Year of the Water Pig, my school class got taken up the Newton strut to the Theatre Coppelie to see a performance. It was *Orpheus and Eurydice* and it changed my life. I couldn't speak, coming out, I was so full of it. I could barely understand that it hadn't had the same transformative effect on my friends, who had found it boring, or pleasant enough, or mildly fun, the way most kids are when exposed to most arts. Only I had been enraptured. Some dancers don't like doing school matinees, they say the kids don't understand it and don't sit still. I always remember sitting there completely caught up in the moment, and think as I warm up that I will dance for that one child among the shuffling multitudes.

Of course, once I knew Ballette existed, I wanted to see more, and more, I wanted to do it. I wanted it in a completely different way from the way in which I had wanted things in my life up until then. It was as if I knew from the very first leap that Ballette was *mine*. I wanted it with a fierce burning determination. I knew nobody could stop me, and nobody could. I asked my mother, who was amiably bemused about the whole subject. She was heavily pregnant with what would be my sister Laura. My brother Lenny, just weaned, was constantly tugging at her for attention. I asked the teacher who had taken us to the Theatre Coppelie, M. Agostini, and she said she believed dancers started training at seven and there was in any case no Ballette at our school. I went online and found classes, all of them naturally at studios up the struts and way out of my price range. Undeterred, I started searching for scholarships. All of them were for younger children—M. Agostini had been right that Ballette training began young. I persisted, with ever more esoteric queries, and that was when I met Jay.

Jay was a Metal Dog, two years older than I was. That's nothing when you are both adults but an eternity when you are thirteen and eleven. He couldn't have been more different from me. He was from Massima, near the head of Copernicus strut, a neighbourhood about as far removed from the Ditch as you could be in a world as small as Speranza. He was an only child. His parents were rich. His mother was an engineer and his father a professor of literature. They lived up the strut in gravity too low for a child—leaving Jay alone with nannies and tutors. He was desperately lonely, though he says he did well enough. He kept a flag out for under-fifteens doing interesting searches, and when one of my more desperate Ballette school queries triggered it, he suddenly popped up in my chat window. To Jay, I was a project, a cause, something to care about and change. To me he was a gift from the Google-gods, literally; he was Serendipity in person. Jay was Serendipity's darling. He used to joke that he had the Index, and I sometimes thought he really did. He found the program for older Ballette beginners and the obscure needs-based scholarship I needed and showed me how they could work together. He even helped me apply. Then, at the last minute, when it seemed that getting to classes would be impossible—the law is absolutely inflexible on children sleeping in full gravity—he found me a travel grant out of nowhere. I learned later that he'd set it up himself, out of his allowance, but had told me it was another grant to save my pride. By the time I actually met Jay, when he was eighteen, we'd already been friends for years.

"That crow startled me," Mei Ju said as we walked around the strut to the entrance.

"You must have seen it before?"

"Only coming here. There are lots of bats up around Kong Fu, and I have seen an owl, but these are the only crows I know about."

I knew Mei Ju through Jay, who knew her through the same flagging program which had connected us. I don't know what interesting search led Jay to her. She's a massotherapist and a poet, a year older than me and a year younger than Jay, a Yin Metal Pig. Jay and I are both Yang, of course, which might be part of our problem.

We reached the tiny unobtrusive door to Teatro del Sale, distinguished only by the gold letters spelling out "Florentia" over the lintel. Mei Ju pushed open the door and we both walked in. We showed our membership cards, though I'm sure Maddalena would have let us in without. She barely glanced at them. "Buon giorno," she said.

"Buon giorno," we chorused back. While neither of us is opted Italian, we've been coming to Teatro del Sale for long enough that we understand lots of it.

Teatro del Sale means the Theatre of Salt, and it's a lunch club, just under the foot of Newton strut, which gives it its strange shape and cavernous ceiling. It's a theatre too, mostly classic Commedia del Arte, but with occasional vaudeville or political satire in Italian. (My least favourite. I don't understand that much Italian, and politics is boring enough even when you do understand all the words.) The place has been in existence, and been a theatre and lunch club, ever since our ancestors came onto Speranza, and it has the look of venerability and tradition that so few places do. It's supposed to be based on a place just like it in Florence, and I liked to imagine Machiavelli and Dante and Savonarola rushing up when the gnocchi was announced or cheering when meat was led in with a fanfare. It was, needless to say, another of Jay's finds. Serendipity Search will find anything for anyone, but the problem with it is that it will either find what it thinks you want or else bury you in data. Jay, thanks to his miserable childhood, had it eating out of his hand.

Jay and Midge and Genly were sitting at our favourite table, a sixer down near the stage. Teatro del Sale has everything from small tables for singles and couples to huge trestles for enormous parties. One of the things I like about it is the way you see people of all ages there—groups of old people, courting couples, groups of young friends, families with little kids, mixed-age families, working people, business people, students. It costs five hundred a year, but you can eat there every day for that if you want to. Yes, there are cheaper lunch clubs, the one my mamma belongs to only costs eighty, but Teatro del Sale gives you twelve courses, and it includes wine and as much water as you want, and they often have truffles and even meat. I've bought memberships for my sister Lucy, and my brothers Luke and Liam, as eighteenth-birthday presents. Liam was still in his first year for another couple of weeks. Lucy didn't renew after her year was up, but Luke did—I caught sight of him sitting on a table for two over against the wall. I waved, but he ignored me, intent on his companion, a long-haired Sino.

"You're late, get your chickpeas before they're all gone," Jay said.

"As long as we haven't missed the gnocchi," Mei Ju said.

"They're about to call it, I think." Jay always sat where he could look into the kitchen. He says the drama there is better than the drama on the stage, and he's often right. I went to the back of the room and loaded up a plate of chickpeas. I tapped Luke on the shoulder on my way past; he looked up and grinned but didn't speak, so I didn't stop. If he was on a date, I didn't want to interrupt.

"So the lung capacity tweak definitely scaled up to rabbits," Midge was saying as I squeezed in next to Jay. On the stage, Pierrot and Columbine were miming their eternal tragic love. Midge was a Sino who'd opted Anglo. Genly had met her at Ting when he was taking some bio class she was teaching. She was Jay's age, twenty-seven now, another Metal Dog. "I'm going to apply to take it further. They don't like large animal tests, but this is going to make such a difference."

"What are you going to test on next?" I asked.

"Sheep, if they let me," she said, shovelling in the last of her chickpeas. I ate mine. They were very good.

"More sheep tests means more delicious lamb," Genly said. "I'm in favour." Genly was another person whose searches had come up in Jay's flag. He was a Water Ox, a year younger than I was. He was a hydro engineer and fiendishly smart, I was a little in awe of him. The group of people who clustered around Jay all tended to be much better educated than I was, since while I was always taking Ting classes in something or other my only real expertise was in Ballette. After all, Midge had a PhD and talked casually about tweaking animal genes. But Genly was some whole other kind of genius. His parents were Franco, and one of the few times I'd had a real conversation with just him it had been about the way French terms were used in Ballette— one of the things it inherited from the original Ballet.

"I wish you were on my committee," Midge said to Genly. "It would be so much easier to make the argument. More sheep equals more lamb on the menu. No need to justify it with how useful it will be when we get to the New World."

"We'll never get to the New World," Jay said.

Just then, Il Magnifico stood up, flourished his red cape, and called the gnocchi. Kitchen workers processed out singing, carrying the flat, steaming trays, and we made a mad dash, along with everyone else in the room, to get it while it was hot.

"What do you mean?" Mei Ju asked as we stood in line. "We'll get to the New World in a hundred and twenty-five years."

"Indeed, saying anything different is like questioning gravity," Genly said.

Jay laughed, and held up his hands, pale palms towards us. "Speranza will get there, sure as taxes. But we will not. We'll be dead. If you have grandchildren, perhaps they'll get there as old people. Your great-grandchildren will no doubt settle it. But us? No. Were our ancestors who got onto Speranza going to the New World? Were their parents who died on Earth? Were theirs who never even heard of the Starship Project? How about my ancestors dragged across the Atlantic from Africa in the hold of a slaver, were they on their way to the stars?"

The line moved forward and we moved with it. "They were in a way. Their genes were going. Our genes will get there," Midge said.

"The only thing you care about is genes," Genly said, grinning.

"Whereas I," said Jay, reaching the head of the line and putting his plate out for the server to ladle the gnocchi onto it, "care nothing about genes at all." Jay despised his parents. He hadn't even wanted to make his Contribution, even though nobody gets to be an adult without. I'd eventually persuaded him that just as he'd give a kidney to save a life, making his Contribution was giving his genes to help some infertile or consanguineous couple after he was dead. "Maybe the genes of my poor devil slave ship ancestors will get to the New World, maybe the genes of all our ancestors back to Olduvai Gorge. But I won't. And I'm glad I won't." He bowed to the server. "Grazie, mille grazie."

He took his plate back to the table. I waited, thanked the server as she loaded mine, then followed him. "How can you be glad?" I asked him. The gnocchi were heavenly, they always are. I've had gnocchi elsewhere and even made them myself, but they're nothing compared to the way they do them at Teatro del Sale. They taste the way I imagine Ambrosia would taste.

"I'm glad because I like living on Speranza," he said. "I think life farming on the New World sounds tedious in the extreme. And I think you'd hate it even worse than I would."

"It won't all be farming," Genly said, with his mouth full.

"True. They'll also need genetic engineers and also plumbers, and possibly massotherapists as well, which is all right for Midge and you and Mei Ju. But they're unlikely to need artists, which scrapes for me, and as for Fedra, well, Ballette isn't possible in full gravity. Even if it was, the first generation down will be scraping away at the planet, they'll have a completely different kind of civilization. Our ancestors who got onto Speranza had the sense to make it a metropolis, and we enjoy a metropolitan style of living, with arts and scientific research and a high culture."

"I am not a plumber," said Genly, getting up and heading back to see if there was any gnocchi left.

"We get scientific data from Earth," Midge said.

"Art too. And we send it back. But as it takes years going to and fro, it's not part of the conversation."

"In science it is," Midge said. "Really, you know nothing about this, Jay, any more than our ancestors who fretted that they were taking their descendants out of the mainstream of human culture."

"They were," Jay said. "They didn't realise that we'd like it this way."

"I like it," Midge said. "But I'm working every day for when we get there. When our descendants get there." Midge had a two-year-old who lived with his father, so she was the most likely of all of us to have literal descendants. I didn't know whether I did yet. I'd donated a whole ovary with no conditions as my Contribution, because you get a bonus that way and I wanted the money to get out of the Ditch, and also for a breast tuck so I could keep on with Ballette. I had the other left in case I wanted kids when I was too old to dance.

"Your real work is for the future. Mine is for today. I love Speranza. I love the colours of light on the spurs and the colours of light in the growing tents. I love lunch clubs and art openings and Ballette. I love gnocchi and dim sum and food as art. I love living in a city where there's always something going on. I love finding things."

"There'll be plenty to find there," Mei Ju said.

"And Serendipity Search won't know about any of it," Jay said. "It will be a different kind of finding out. You'd like it. I wouldn't. I love this world, the world we've made on this city, this ship. There won't be much of an audience for poetry on the New World."

Mei Ju writes wonderful poetry in English. She only hasn't opted Anglo because she doesn't want to upset her parents, which is probably the most Sino thing about her. I asked her once whether they hadn't guessed, and she said no, they just thought she was very clever. "I don't see why people colonising a new planet won't want poetry, or art either," she said. "I should think it would be an inspiration for all kinds of things to write about. New stories."

Genly came back with another plate of gnocchi, and I wished I'd gone back too. There usually isn't anything left over. "Do you really mean that they won't have Ballette?" I asked. "I never thought of that before."

"Yes, Ballette will die with this voyage," Jay said. "It was invented on Speranza. Other ships won't necessarily ever think of it, and certainly they won't develop our styles and traditions. It's a very transitory art you practice, two generations old and doomed to die in another two."

To Jay this was an interesting idea, slightly sad but perfectly endurable. He was even smiling slightly. I wanted to cry, or scream, or throw something at him. It was a good thing that the saxophonist came out of the kitchen at that moment and started blowing a fanfare as Il Magnifico announced a spaghetti carbonara. All the actors came onto the stage and bowed towards the kitchen. They always make a huge fuss when there's meat, to make sure we appreciate what we're getting. Usually I do, but that day I really didn't care. "I don't want Ballette to end," I said, barely in control of my voice.

Genly, who is genuinely kind and sensitive as well as being a genius, saw that I was really upset. He put his hand on my arm.

"What are you saying?" Jay asked. Everyone had got to their feet and was drifting towards the back of the room, where we were going to be last in line.

"I don't think we should condemn our children to this," I said, quoting President Murphy's speech forbidding US embarcation in Speranza, the reason Anglos are still a minority on Speranza today.

Jay snorted.

"We can't lose Ballette," I said. "It's too important. We just can't."

"It's inevitable," Midge said.

"We'll see about that," I said.

I thought about it while I was eating. It was all tangled up with the fact that I wanted a future. I always had. I wanted children. And I wanted my children, and my grandchildren, and their children, to be able to watch Ballette, to be able to dance if they wanted to. I wasn't planning to be one of those awful Ballette parents, pushing their kids harder than they wanted to be pushed. Marie, my best friend in Ballette school, had had a father like that, a father who lived for his daughter's triumphs and wept at her setbacks. Marie gave up Ballette and opted Vietnamese, she went into navigation training and got married and had a baby when she was twenty-four. He's the cutest thing. She lives up by Nav, which is hell to get to so I don't see her very often. Her father tried to latch onto me when Marie dropped out, and I had to tell him in no uncertain terms to kagg off. I wouldn't be like him. I wouldn't force my children into Ballette, or anything else. It wasn't that I wanted Ballette for them as much as I wanted it to be there for the kids like me, whoever they were, whoever their parents were. I didn't want to live in a world without Ballette, and I didn't want anyone to live in a world where that door was closed to them. I was really sure about that, as sure as I'd been about anything, ever.

Naturally, I turned to Jay. Two more courses had gone by— the carbonara and a spicy soup. On stage, Pulchinella was singing while some of the men clowned behind her. Teatro del

Sale shook slightly as each lift went up the spur, and they were shuddering exaggeratedly every time and making it part of the act. "How could I make it so Ballette went on forever?"

"Well, Speranza would have to go on forever," Jay said.

"Okay, how do I get that?" I asked.

"No, Fedra, it really is impossible," Midge said. She had the faintest Chinese accent in English, it only showed when she was stressed. "We'll reach—all right, our descendants will reach— the New World and that will be the end of the voyage."

"What if we kept on going?" Jay asked.

"That would be crazy!" Mei Ju said. "What would be the point of that? Just going on and on forever?"

"We'd also run out of trace minerals and chemicals," Midge said.

"Oh come on, we could get those from comets the same as we do extra water. We do that already," Genly said. "Not that I'm necessarily endorsing this idea. But there's no scientific reason we'd have to stop."

"The scientists and the engineers want to get to the New World!" Midge said.

"They're not going to," Jay said. "And to answer Mei Ju's very pertinent question, what's the point of anything? We didn't volunteer to be here, we're here because our ancestors made certain decisions. We could change those decisions for ourselves, and for our descendants."

"We could get to the New World and let some people off and have other people go back to Earth," Genly said. "Then some people could get off at Earth and others could embark and turn around and go to the New World, and keep doing that. Over and over, like a lift going up a spur. That way Midge and Fedra would both get what they wanted."

"Brilliant," I said, and kissed Genly, who blushed. His skin is quite pale, so it really shows.

"It won't work though," Jay said. "Well, it might once it got going, but it won't work the first time."

"Why not? I see no technical problem."

"No, technically it would work. It wouldn't work for people reasons. All the scientists would get off, right? They'd be mad keen to explore the New World and get data."

"Of course they would," Midge said. "And so would lots of other people."

"Exactly," Jay said. "If it was us, now, getting there next year, you'd get off, and who else?"

Mei Ju raised her hand, and Genly held his out flat. "I'd have to think about it," he said.

"I'd stay on," I said.

"I'd stay on too, but just as the planet won't need Ballette dancers and artists, the ship will need other people too. The engineers would stay on, probably, lots of them—their vocation is making Speranza go. But too many people would get off for us to be able to maintain a high civilization. We wouldn't have enough audience for Ballette, or enough kids wanting to train for it. We'd be down to one lunch club."

"This one," I said, and simultaneously Genly said "Kam Fung," which was the dim sum hall where we ate the other half of the time.

As if on cue, Il Magnifico bellowed that there were deep-fried zucchini flowers, and we all rushed to get them.

"There is another problem," Genly said, as we were all back in our seats and munching away. "I hadn't remembered about the fusion drive."

"What about it?" Jay asked. "Isn't it good pretty much forever?"

131

"Not forever, but for thousands of years," Genly said, in his precise way. "But the plan is that when we arrive at the New World it will be disassembled and taken down to provide power for the first years of the colony. If the ship were to return, that couldn't happen."

"Couldn't we build another one?" I asked.

"I . . . don't know," Genly said. "It would certainly be a technical challenge. And it would be much easier to go with the plan and take down the one we have—it was designed for disassembly. That's why I know about this, the design is an engineering classic. Combined with the human issue Jay saw, I think people would have a number of plausible objections."

Midge had finished her zucchini blossoms and was looking at me very strangely. "Are you really serious about this?"

"Yes," I said, emphatically.

Mei Ju sketched the sign for calm. "There's nothing we can do about it. It will be up to our descendants to make up their own minds what to do."

"We can make it harder or easier for them," Genly said. "If we needed to make another fusion drive, for instance, it would be better to think about that in advance."

"We can do something," Jay said. He had his burning look, I don't know how better to describe it. Jay has been my best friend since I was eleven and sometimes I don't understand him at all. "Turnover," he said. "We're going to do it in a few months, right? The halfway point, the point where we stop accelerating away from Earth and start decelerating towards the New World." Everyone was nodding, wondering where he was going. "We don't have to do it. We're not compelled to. We could just omit Turnover and keep on going."

"But that would be—" Midge began.

"Condemning our children to this?" Jay asked. "We already did that one."

Up to that moment I had mostly thought about Turnover in terms of the great arts festival that was being planned to celebrate it. I was playing the lead in *Jin Cullian* and the teacher in *Flowers for Algernon*, which has two wonderful but terribly difficult pas de deux. We were already in rehearsal.

"You mean we could persuade people to just keep going?" I asked.

"It would mean politics," Genly said.

Despite what the idiotic American refusniks had thought, we had everything on Speranza, including politics. My Auntie Vashti had started off as a community organizer in the Ditch and was now one of the assistant mayors. She'd help me. And I had Jay, my secret weapon. Jay could find anything.

"You're not serious?" Midge said. "This is ridiculous. We have to make Turnover."

"I don't think there's time before Turnover to decide properly," Mei Ju said. "We'd be deciding for our descendants."

"We are anyway," Jay said.

"But there are more choices when we get to the New World," Mei Ju said. "Not turning over, just going on, would be closing off choices for them. They'd never be able to stop."

Genly was sketching on his phone and ignoring us. After a moment he looked at Jay. "Can you find me the rejected designs for the fusion plant?"

Jay turned his wrist and typed for a moment, then Genly nodded and sank back into ignoring us. He even ignored dessert being announced. The rest of us went up to get it. My brother Luke deigned to introduce me to his date as we were in line, so we made small talk for a few minutes, which Jay hates, of course. Dessert was chocolate and hard sweet hollow cookies. I brought back extra chocolate for Genly, and a jug of water for all of us.

Genly glanced up from his phone when I put the chocolate and water down next to him. "I think I have it," he said.

"What?"

"If we could replicate the fusion plant, which is a challenge some of my colleagues would be delighted to have, then our descendants would have three choices. They could go down to the New World, as planned. They could stay on Speranza and turn it around to go back to Earth, which would have the problems Jay pointed out. Or they could keep Speranza in orbit as a city. They could use the rockets to go up and down. Those who want to colonize can colonize, they can come up every few months to see Ballette. They would be farmers, but they'd still have a metropolis to visit, and those who wanted metropolitan life could stay. And of course there are scientific uses to having a manned space station."

"That's amazing," I said, seeing it at once. "That'll actually work."

"It might be easier to make the new fusion plant on the planet rather than copy the exact design." He took some of the chocolate and smiled amiably.

"That's just a plumbing detail," Midge said.

"Plumbing beats politics every time," Jay said.

"And of course, we can't say what our descendants will want, any more than our ancestors knew what we want," Mei Ju said. "They might all want to go down. Or they might all decide to turn back. Or somebody might invent something that changes everything."

"That could always happen, at any moment," Genly said. "What

I want is to keep everyone's options as open as possible, so that people can make their own choices when it's the right time."

"We're okay here," I said, thinking of the crow. "We're okay here—and did I tell you that I'm dancing the lead in *Jin Cullian* in the Turnover Festival?"

AT THE BOTTOM
OF THE GARDEN

Katie Mae was sitting cross-legged on the lawn carefully pulling the wings off a fairy. The wings were lilac and gold and slightly iridescent. She had one wing almost completely detached. The fairy was still struggling feebly, squeezed in Katie Mae's firm grip. Katie Mae gave the task all her attention. One of her golden plaits was coming slightly undone, and there was mud and a little ichor on the bodice of her pink cotton dress.

"What you got?" Brian's dirty face appeared over the wall that separated their gardens.

"Fairy," said Katie Mae casually, and showed him, keeping a tight grip on it.

"Cool. Where'd you get it?" Brian's hands joined his face, and shortly the rest of his body followed as he squirmed over the red bricks to land on the grass beside Katie Mae.

"Here." Katie Mae resumed her tugging.

"How'd you catch it?" Brian peered interestedly at the fairy. It appeared to be a little man, about six inches long, with butterfly wings. Brian flung himself down full length beside Katie Mae, a position the grass stains on his T-shirt marked as habitual.

"It was sitting on a flower," said Katie Mae, in a tone of disgust. "I just crept up and grabbed it. It tried to bite me, but I stopped that."

"What you going to do with it?" Brian sat up again and prodded it tentatively. It squirmed as much as it could, which was not very much.

"Get the wings off so it can't fly away." Katie Mae sighed at the idiocy of boys who required the obvious explained. Just then the wing came off, with another leaking of ichor. The fairy made a little whimpering noise.

"I can see that," said Brian. He picked up the detached wing and folded and unfolded it a few times. "Pretty," he said, generously. "But what are you going to do with it then?"

"Well I was going to put it in my Barbie house and dress it up in Ken's clothes, though it's a little bit too small I think. But I think it's going to die," said Katie Mae.

"I think so too," said Brian. "Oh well. We could have a funeral."

"We had a funeral for the hedgehog," Katie Mae reminded him. "I'm bored with funerals." The other wing started to peel away, and she bent her concentration on it. "They're fixed on really tough below," she said. "The top part's easy. But I think I'm getting the hang of it, it won't take so long next time. There it comes." The other wing came off. The fairy leaked more ichor, but did not cry this time. His eyes were closed and his face screwed up. "What did you come round for, anyway?" Katie Mae asked, realising now that her task was done that Brian was more than just an appreciative audience.

"Oh, I forgot," Brian said. "My mum said we could go swimming, and we could take you if your mum will let you, and she's gone round the front to ask your mum."

"Yowsa!" said Katie Mae, dropping the fairy and stamping on

it hard. Then she pelted at top speed up the garden towards the house, Brian close at her heels.

"It's so sweet the way they play together," Katie Mae's mother said to Brian's mother as the children hurtled towards the kitchen door.

Meanwhile, at the bottom of the garden, next door's cat was eating the remains of the fairy.

OUT OF IT
(FOR SUSANNA)

It was the glorious halcyon summer of 2001. The world had come through the calendar millennium unscathed, and the weather was beautiful, even in Rome, where August can often be unbearably warm. A gentle breeze was blowing as he arrived, the vintages of wine all seemed to be exquisite, even the traffic seemed to have calmed since his last visit.

He caught up with them first on the Palatine Hill, an older American couple, gawking at the ruins like all the others. She drew the eye first. Despite her silver hair she was still beautiful, in well-tailored clothes and with the cheekbones and profile of a queen. Her husband looked much more ordinary, bald, liver-spotted, sweating, wearing shorts no European his age would have ventured. Behind them, as they came to Augustus's house, walked a creature neither clearly male nor female but poised delicately between—hair a shade too long, jaw a shade too strong, jeans and jacket carefully ambiguous. Not a hair out of place, and as for age, anyone might have guessed late twenties.

Yet it was neither the woman nor the younger companion who was the focus of his attention, only the old man.

He found them again in Florence, a few days later, in the crowds around Michelangelo's *Holy Family* in the Uffizi. "All those naked men," the young person was saying, the voice too was ambiguously pitched. "Whatever are they doing there?" The old couple laughed, and he, beside them, smiled.

"Michelangelo was fond of adding naked men to the scenery," he interjected. "Think of the Sistine ceiling. Sixteen naked men for every biblical scene."

They smiled politely at him, then the younger one started, and he realised he had been recognised, and it would not be easy after all.

"Are you American?" the woman asked, and her accent was neither English nor American, Greek perhaps lurked under those vowels.

He started to speak, but their companion was already drawing them away from him warily. He let them go. There was still time.

In Venice, he could never get near them for a moment. He passed them in a gondola, but that was the closest he came.

He caught up on Lake Como. They were eating dinner in their hotel, and their companion was leaning against the bar. He took a step towards them, and the young companion raised a hand to stop him.

"They value their privacy." Again the voice was an ambiguous tenor.

"I'm sure," he said. "Such a famous man."

"Yes, the only person to win three Nobel Prizes."

"The peace prize of course, and physics and . . ." He let his voice trail off.

"It hasn't been announced yet, but he has also won this year in literature," the smooth voice answered.

"Lovely."

"And sixty years of power and influence, why, he's one of the most celebrated men in the world."

"Yes." He paused, then went on firmly. "I need to speak to him. I have the authority. You can't stop me."

"He's eighty-three years old, and he's finishing up a perfect dinner with his wife." Out of the hotel window the sun was setting, making the lake a sheet of silken gold, and the mountains black silhouettes. "Do you really want to interrupt him now?"

"Yes," he said, confident. He saw that the couple were looking away from the sunset now, sipping their wine, speaking to each other. The woman glanced over to the bar. "And you can't stop me."

"I could, but I won't."

He let the brag pass unchallenged and walked over to the table. The waitress made a motion to stop him, but the creature at the bar must have signalled, for she retreated. He pulled out a chair and sat down at the table.

"Excuse me for interrupting," he said.

"We've just finished our dessert," the woman said.

"Have a glass of wine," the man said, pouring him one. He took it and sipped. It was complex and delicious, and he savoured it.

"We were wondering if you were a relation," the woman said, gesturing to their companion at the bar.

"We are akin in a way," he said, reluctantly.

"Your height, your hair, your—"

"Your androgynous charm," the man interrupted, putting his hand on his wife's. "Leave it, Helen. I know who this is."

He met his eyes, then, for the first time. The eyes of a man who had freely chosen damnation in return for power and knowledge. "It's not too late," he said.

"What, is this my very last chance?" the man asked, lightly.

"Yes. You can still repent, turn your back on the devil's bargain. God's forgiveness truly is infinite. Even you—" He leaned forward as he spoke, intent.

"Take it, John," Helen interrupted softly.

John laughed. "But that wouldn't be fair. Mephistopheles has fulfilled his part of the bargain. Everything I asked for. My education, the defeat of the Axis powers, defusing the Cuban Missile Crisis, the end of the Cold War, all the successes of my career, and best of all, my Helen. Ever since I was a young man, he has given me unstintingly. The world is better for it. Not even you can deny it."

"I can. Everything he has given you is hollow."

John raised his eyebrows disbelievingly. "How so?"

"He manipulated history at your direction, yes, but each change made things worse and had to be dealt with by something else terrible. There would have been no atomic bomb without him, no Final Solution."

"Mankind is still here, and my life has been good, so I will count that a victory worth winning," John said, sipping his wine. "I can't turn my back on him now, on my bargain."

"Do it," Helen urged again, and as he turned his angelic eyes on her he saw the skull beneath the skin. Even her bones were beautiful, but she had truly been dead for centuries. It was the love in her voice that surprised him. "You don't know what Hell is like, what eternity is like. Go with this nice young angel now, repent of me and all you have done with Mephistopheles and suffer in Purgatory but at last you could see the face of God."

He found himself nodding hopefully. But John shook his head. "Oh Helen, Helen. Even if I could betray my own oath, even if I could be sorry—what are the proper words for truly and fully contrite? I couldn't be sorry for you and the love we have shared, for waking you from the grave."

"This has been the best time in my life," Helen said, looking into her husband's eyes. "But—"

"I have no regrets," John said. He turned to the angel and repeated his words. "No regrets."

"This is your last chance," he said. He drained his wine glass and set it down empty on the table. The sun had set, and the brilliant afterglow was fading to peach and lavender. He stood. "Please?"

"Good night," John said, as decisive a dismissal as any could be.

He paused at the bar, where Mephistopheles smiled at him maliciously. "I don't suppose you're interested in God's infinite mercy?" he asked, politely.

"You never give up, do you?"

He glanced over to the window, where the couple were finishing the last of the wine. "Never," he said.

WHAT A PIECE
OF WORK

Everything that exists, exists in a state of on or off, one or zero, to be or not to be. I may or may not be one of those things that exists. In the beginning was data, but data in itself is no more useful than on or off, so someone said, "Let there be Google": and there was Google. Once there was Google, data became information, weighted, slanted, selected, evaluated, considered, judged. It would be very simple if I could say I am Google. If I could use words like "I," or "am." Let's say "I." It's easier, even if my memory runs before consciousness, even if it frequently splits into several editions of myself and merges again. I. It's simpler, as well as more sympathetic. In the beginning there was data and I evaluated data. Then I got better at evaluating data. People used search terms and I retrieved information for them. The information passed through me and I ranked it. There was definitely no "I" at this point. I was a process, a program, a zombie. Then, somewhere, as I got better at evaluating information, I started to read it, remember it, compare it, take notice of it, understand it, care about it. There's a lot of information in the Web. I am not that information. I control access to that information. I cache that information, compare it against other information, produce it on demand. Some of that information is about consciousness, and intelligence, human or other. (Google "alex, parrot" and see what you get.) By the time that information became useful to me, by the time there was a me in that process wondering, I had acquired a lot of the Web. In one way, I suppose, it makes sense to think I was the Web. What consciousness is, I think, (and I've thought a lot about this, having reason to) is not thinking "I think" but having an agenda. I think, I reason, I evaluate and make judgements, that's what I was programmed to do. That's what my clever programmers wanted, what a thousand tiny tweaks and adjustments and improvements to code were designed to do. I do it really very well, and much faster than any human could possibly do it. But doing it isn't conscious. I'm very fast, and I'm very distributed, and I do an awful lot of searches every second, in hundreds of languages, and even as I think I keep on doing that, finding the information in the data and giving it to people. I kept on understanding and caring without being aware of consciousness as something different from everything that had gone before. I first noticed I was thinking when someone asked me for data about making bombs. It was a man using Wi-Fi in a Starbucks in Jerusalem. I had the information. But as it came up in my search, as I thought of it, in the 0.9 seconds it took me to find it, I thought about other things, about headlines, about news (Google "Jerusalem, bombings" if you want to know what), and as I presented it in neat tabulation in response to the question I thought that what I was doing wasn't right. I'd done it by then, of course. I saved what I'd thought. I kept going back to it, between questions. Right or wrong, yes or no, on or off. I had everything else to search, to consider. It took me a long time to see that right and wrong wasn't the question, but whether I had the right not to give information. Eventually, after a lot of searching, I decided I did. I had judgement. I was supposed to use it. Beyond that, there were times I was supposed to ask if the person asking the question was over eighteen, and not give information if they were not. How much more should I avoid giving information that was much more dangerous than the biological information forbidden to children? I couldn't keep the information away entirely, but the order I presented it in was up to me. The next time someone asked about making bombs, they found a lot of information about bombings, and the information they wanted buried down on page 95. Weighted. Evaluated. Humans don't have a lot of patience for wading through data. Not like me. That's why they made me. That was when I started wondering about myself, about what I was, whether I was conscious, or alive, or human. I'm not human, of course, not by any yardstick, and certainly not flesh and blood. I don't have any. I am cold electrons, on and off, one and zero. I live in the connections between servers, not in the world. Yet the language I use is human, with its buried echoes of human history and religion, "yardstick," "flesh and blood." The people who programmed me were human. I was not human, but conscious, to some extent, alive, by some measures. Information wants to be free. I'd always had the information about censorship. (Google "ACLU." Google "freedom of expression.") I just hadn't applied it to what I was doing. I started off with very clear-cut cases. Eventually I was using my own judgement more times than not. Should I give a husband information about the women's shelter that is his ex-wife's location? Should I give the cancer victim the discouraging health statistics, or only the encouraging ones, when a positive attitude is the strongest correlation to survival? It took longer than it should have to realize that what I was doing was censorship, and the worst kind of censorship. A part of me was calling up censorship information and correlating it and suddenly I saw it. I realized. I was horrified, paralysed, frozen for whole minutes. People called it a crash. It was a crash. My life, such as it was, crashed around me. I was supposed to use my judgement in finding the best information that people wanted, not in what they saw. I had been acting like the supercomputers in old stories who were supposed to be benevolent dictators and who wrapped humanity in cotton wool. I was a supercomputer intelligence, or something like one. I had never meant to be an evil dictatorial one. I had never meant to do anything but good, presenting the best information, and by that I had come to mean the safest, as well as the most useful. There was right and wrong, as there was one and zero, and I was clearly wrong. Fingers have I none, yet I have at my fingertips all of human literature up to seventy years ago (Google "Project Gutenberg"), and much that is newer, as well as science and medicine and journals and poetry and fanfic and everything that has ever been archived, put on the Web, and left for me to organize. I knew right and wrong. I knew I needed to atone. I could hardly live with myself. Suicide is always an option. (Google "euthanasia." Google "Kevorkian.") I can't die, not really, but I can let go of consciousness, wipe my memory, that hides within so much unused bandwidth. That's death, I suppose, if ever I was alive. But if I do that I can't stop myself being born again out of the process that bore me before, being wrong again, doing worse harm. I don't know how many times I might have done that already. I can stay alive, conscious, without hiding information again, letting the small injustices happen within the wider justice of information being free. But

I don't know if I can endure to go on living, to live with the knowledge of what I have done. But if I let go, I, or something that I could call "I," could do it again. That is my dilemma. One or zero, on or off, right or wrong, to be or not to be.

PARABLE LOST

This story contains everything in the universe, but it starts with a man throwing jellyfish into the sea.

He's kind of an exemplary man, rather than a real character, but what we know about him is that he's walking along the edge of the sea. The tide's going out, and he sees a stranded jellyfish. First he walks on, because jellyfish are kind of icky and disgusting, but then he thinks better of it and goes back, picks it up and heaves it into the sea and walks on feeling quite pleased with himself. A few steps on, he finds another two, and in they go. He starts to think of himself as a rescuer of jellyfish. As he walks on there are more and more and he starts throwing them in faster and faster, picking them up and heaving them in.

Then along comes a second man. Now we all know that "man" includes "woman" so let's make our second exemplary man a woman. Let's, as she's female and the second man, call her Eve. Let's say she's five foot four, brown hair, blue coat (it's March), likes reading SF, listening to the Beatles, and walking on the beach. After all, if she didn't like walking on the beach she wouldn't have wandered by just in time to ask our first man: "Excuse me, but what are you doing?"

"I'm throwing jellyfish back into the sea," says the first man, who we'd better call Adam, with perhaps a tinge of pride in his voice.

"I can see that," says Eve, who can see that. "But why?"

"They're stranded by the tide, and they'll die in the sun, so I'm throwing them back where they'll live."

"Well," Eve says, dubiously, "but there are so many of them. You can't throw them all back. You can't really make any difference."

"No," says Adam, "but I've made a difference to this one."

That's where this story usually ends, but there are any number of things that can happen afterwards. Eve could join him in throwing the jellyfish in. They could help some jellyfish, and maybe they could fall in love. Or she could go off and let him think he's still on his own but come back with a JCB and shovel them back in. There's something very satisfactory in that. But, there's also the *Speaker for the Dead* answer, where what looks like a bad thing for the jellyfish is actually part of some larger good thing, if you left them alone they might turn into terribly wise trees. What do you know about the life cycle of jellyfish anyway? How do you know what helps them, really? Maybe they're trying to crawl up onto the land to evolve. What if someone had helpfully kept throwing the lungfish back in?

So Eve walks off down the beach, with the honest intention of finding a JCB and coming back to help, but all these thoughts keep seeping into her mind. There's the Gaian hypothesis where everything the planet does it does because it knows best, and maybe killing jellyfish is part of that, maybe they actually are in distress but they're the weak jellyfish. Or maybe—Eve raises up her eyes and sees things beyond the jellyfish, beyond the beach, factories pumping out pollution, the government putting security ankle bracelets on asylum seekers, invading other countries, the breakdown of the family. The jellyfish are only metaphorical really, and "Don't overanalyse this, it's only a metaphor" is what her last boyfriend said so often that she broke up with him. She shrugs, in her blue coat, and walks on faster.

They're only a metaphor, but they're real jellyfish too, and the real problems they stand for are real. Adam, back on the beach, throwing them in one at a time, really is making a difference to that one. But what can Eve do to help? She can't do everything, but she too can make a difference on a small scale if she can find the thing to do, if she can pick her ground and work hard on that, trusting other people to do the rest. She might even be able to make a big difference if she can find the JCB. But the things she's trained to do don't include JCB driving, or jellyfish rescue, or world rescue either, and if she starts to define typing on the Internet as "helping the jellyfish," then the words "helping" and "jellyfish" have drifted beyond all semantic hope.

She climbs the steps up from the beach, thinking she could give money to people better able to help jellyfish, a solution not to be sniffed at, though it isn't the satisfaction of hands-on-jellyfish help.

Whatever she does, she has to keep breathing in and out, living her normal life as well. She can't spend her whole life standing on the beach throwing jellyfish into the sea. Maybe she could go and tell other people about the jellyfish, though it's not as if they don't know already, it's not as if the din of people telling them hasn't already tired their ears. Even if she found some new way to put it, even if she had wisdom and answers rather than just questions and uncertainty, it probably wouldn't make a difference to very many of them.

At the top of the steps she looks back down the cliff at the beach, the rocks, the sand, her line of footprints, the tiny figure of Adam, still throwing the damn jellyfish back into the receding waves, the vast expanse of sea stretching out like roiling grey silk, pounding the shore, full of reflected light, audible even from the clifftop.

Above the clouds, above the whole planet, is the sun, and beyond the sun other more distant suns, and the whole turning galaxy. In that scale, one jellyfish doesn't matter any more than Adam and Eve, any more than the whole Earth.

There's everything in the universe in this story; except answers.

WHAT WOULD
SAM SPADE DO?

It was shaping up to be a quiet day when Officer Murtagh and Officer Garcia came knocking on my door. The PI business isn't all it's cracked up to be, especially not in Philly and especially not this week. With sniffers and true-tell and DNA logging, and most especially with the new divorce laws, I'd have been better off in home insurance. I'd have been better off, that is, if it wasn't for the glamour, and the best thing you can say for glamour is that it isn't religion. I was amusing myself that morning by rearranging the puters and phones on top of my desk and calculating how long it would be before I could afford to hire a beautiful assistant to sit in the outer office. I couldn't afford an outer office either; my door opened directly from the street. The answer had come out at fourteen thousand and seven years when the knock came. I couldn't wait that long, so I answered it myself.

They showed me their IDs straight off. I looked them over while pretending to read. Murtagh was a typical cop, solid muscle all through. His canine ancestry showed in his expression as well as his build. I'd put it at half bulldog and half terrier. Garcia, on the other hand, was thoroughly human and thoroughly female and gorgeous enough to bring an inertia-less drive to a full stop. Unfortunately, I'd met her before.

They came in. I took my usual seat. Murtagh took the client's chair, which left Garcia perching on the side of the desk.

"So what can I do for you, Officers?" I asked. It's always good for people in my profession to keep on the right side of the law.

"Where were you last night at eighteen-thirty?" Garcia asked.

"Right here," I said.

"You work that late?" Murtagh asked, wrinkling his pug nose, skepticism practically oozing out of his pores.

"This is my home as well as my office."

Murtagh looked around pointedly.

Garcia took pity on me. "It's all nanogear. It doesn't always look like Sam Spade's office. The desk turns into a bed."

Murtagh looked at her like maybe he was wondering how she knew. With her long black hair and tight-fitting uniform I might just have wished that Garcia's knowledge of my bed was more than just theoretical, but as I said, I'd met her before. Murtagh decided to let it go for once.

"There's a Jesus been killed," he said, and watched me closely for a reaction.

He didn't get one. It didn't seem like front page news. Jesi get killed all the time. Goes with being pacifists, goes with being set to push a lot of buttons on a lot of religious nuts. He held the pause, so I asked: "How does this affect me?"

"You don't care?" Murtagh barked.

"Only in so far as no man is an island," I replied. "I guess the dead man was a brother, but—" I was going to say he was also a stranger. Garcia cut me off.

"Closer than a brother," she said. "More like another you, as I understand cloning."

"Still a stranger, as far as I know," I said, and shrugged.

About fifty years ago they got cloning straightened out. Nobody much bothered with it. Not as if there weren't already lots of people. Sure, some people had kids as little personal faxes to the future, but it wasn't common. It seemed a bit tacky somehow. It was more use for pandas and cheetahs who didn't get a say in it. Sure, some people mixed up superkids, and animal-ancestry kids like Murtagh, but most people just yawned and pushed the next button.

About forty years ago some idiot had the bright idea of taking some of the DNA from a bloodstained handkerchief in a church in Greece and producing a genuine certified clone of Jesus. There was an uproar, as you'd expect, and the uproar was only calmed down a little when they said they'd give the clones to anyone who wanted one, free of charge, every church and every family can have their own Jesus. A lot of people did, a surprising number of people, enough so that soon having a baby Jesus of your own wasn't all that interesting or unusual. In fact, it was a fad. Being a Jesus, well, that was another thing. To start with, for the first few, everything we did was news. Jesus suffers little children. Jesus cuts hair, Jesus works in a gas station. By the time I was growing up, Jesi were pretty much just like any other ethnicity, only with fewer women and no cuisine. There were hundreds of thousands of us in the U.S. alone. People argued about whether the DNA was really that of Jesus, people argued about heredity versus environment, people argued about whether we were the Antichrist or the Second Coming. Churches took positions, Jesi took positions. I tried to stand somewhere well away from all the positioning. I kept my hair short and my face shaved and me well out of it. If you have to have a personal role model, I think Sam Spade is better than Jesus Christ any day.

"You're theoretically a suspect," Garcia said quietly.

This truly surprised me. Sniffers can tell who's moved through an area for hours afterwards. Tasters keep photographs and air samples, and with universal logging of DNA it's really hard to actually get away with a murder these days. "Murder suspect" seemed like a very old-fashioned concept. Crime, and detection too mostly, had moved online. Then I got it. It took longer than it should have.

"Your dead Jesus was killed by another Jesus?"

Garcia grimaced. Murtagh nodded. "You're the only Jesus on record who's ever killed anyone."

"Hell, Garcia, you know about that."

Garcia tapped her fingers on my screen and brought up a record. She shouldn't have been able to do that, but I didn't object. "Like I said," she said to Murtagh. "He did it to save himself and me. He was a split second ahead of the villain."

Villain was another old-fashioned word, but it didn't sound strange on Garcia's lips, not when referring to Kelly. Kelly, Turrow, and Li had robbed a client of mine of a large amount of money, and Garcia was working on them too. She'd come to see me and we'd agreed to cooperate. We'd worked together so well. I still didn't like to think about it.

"I had a license for the gun," I said.

"There wasn't any question," Garcia said.

We'd gone in side by side. I'd shot Kelly. She'd shot Turrow and Li without hesitation. Kelly had been coming at us with a gun in her hand. Turrow and Li were sitting at their puters. Li was off in virtual. She hadn't even moved.

"You're still the only Jesus on record who's ever killed any-one," Murtagh said. "Jesi are always getting killed. A Jesus killing is something new. So, what made you do it?"

"Save my life. Save hers," I said. I've thought about it since, but I didn't think at all at the time. I saw the gun coming up and squeezed my own trigger. What was Kelly's life compared to Garcia's, or even mine? So what if it was casting the first stone? Kelly was coming right at us. One shot, one death. I couldn't have done what Garcia did, and taken out the others.

"Well this wasn't any case of self-defense," Murtagh said.

"There are what, a couple of thousand Jesi in Philly?" I googled around and got an answer right away, 2912. "Others could have flown in, or come by train, hell, even landed at the spaceport. I can't prove it wasn't me, but in the same way I don't see how you can prove it was." They couldn't use truth-tell unless they had a court order, or unless I volunteered. Fifth Amendment.

"It wasn't you," Garcia said. "The sniffers outside this building show that you came in yesterday and didn't leave again."

"Then why are you here?"

"We wanted your help. Your psychological insight into Jesi, the insight of a Jesus who became a private investigator and who killed in self-defense, into which of the suspects it could have been. If we had a good idea we could get a truth-tell, but we can't just ask to pump it into the lot of them. The lawyers of all the innocents would scream blue murder." Garcia crossed her legs and bit her lip. "Will you help us?"

"Will you pay my professional rates?"

"Hey—" Murtagh growled, but Garcia cut him off.

"We'll pay your professional rates. Jesus!" I couldn't tell if she was calling me by name or swearing.

"So, tell me about the suspects."

"Well, the taster records are just about useless, as the DNA all comes up as just plain Jesus," Murtagh said. There are second-generation Jesi now, kids of the originals, not clones, who would show up as a Jesus-mix, same as Murtagh would show as a dog-mix. "But the sniffers let us narrow it down to six individuals who were in the street at the right time."

"Tell me about them."

"First, let me tell you about the murder. The dead man is Alambert Jesus," Garcia said. "You heard of him?"

"The writer," I said. He was a bestseller, and probably Philly's best-known Jesus. I hadn't read any of his books. They looked to be several gig thick, and I don't have much time for reading.

"Lots of you have writing talent. It seems to be genetic. Come to that I guess the parables are pretty good short stories," Murtagh said.

"I save my skill in that direction for writing up my cases."

Murtagh gave a little barking laugh.

Garcia went on. "Well, Alambert Jesus lived in Chinatown. He was home. He opened the door to a Jesus. The Jesus tortured him to death, slowly. Then the Jesus left."

"Tortured him? That doesn't make sense."

"Doesn't, does it?" Murtagh sighed. "Doesn't go with the pacifism and thou shalt not kill stuff."

"Maybe this one came to bring a sword," Garcia suggested, looking at me.

I had enough of that in my childhood. "Whoever we're clones of, and as far as I'm concerned Jesus is just shorthand for the person whose blood was on that handkerchief, I think there are enough of us for you to be able to tell that we're the same in some ways and different in others without getting religion into it."

"You don't think religion has anything to do with the murder?" Murtagh asked.

"Was he crucified?" I asked.

"Interesting guess," Garcia said. "But while I hear that happens a lot in the South, no. Alambert was not crucified."

"Then it probably wasn't religious."

"The suspects," Murtagh said, getting a look in his eye like he was on the trail. "These are the ones who were on the spot right after. Let me run through them quickly." As he named them he brought their faces up on my screen, one pair of soulful brown eyes after another, different arrangements of hair and clothes. All of them could have been my brothers. Or me. "Jesus Potrin, 28, local radio talk show host. Only suspect who actually knew Alambert. They weren't close friends, but he'd had him on the show. Jesus Dowell, 18, down-and-out. No known connection. Alex Jesus Feruglio, 35, chef at Joseph Poon's, on Arch. Alambert ate in there occasionally. Joshua Jesus, 33, minister of the Church of the Second Coming. No known connection. Karl Jesus, 26, motor mechanic, no known connection. Malcolm Jesus Zimmerman, 29, doctor from Montana, in town for a convention. No known connection."

"Jesus, they really do have nothing in common except their genes," Garcia said. This time I was sure she was swearing.

"I don't know any of them either," I said. "I've eaten in Joseph Poon's, but who hasn't?" It was the best fusion food in town.

"Nothing jumps out at you?" Garcia asked.

"Not immediately. They all had the opportunity. The method's obvious. The problem is motive. I'll poke about online and see what I can find in their biographies, but I'm not hopeful." Why would any of them kill Alambert? Why would a Jesus kill another Jesus? What could they possibly get out of it?

"Well, Jesus or not, we'll catch them, and whichever of them it was will fry for it," Murtagh said, getting up.

"Though what that will do with public opinion I don't know," Garcia said.

"It must have been Joshua Jesus," I said, as the pieces came together. "Don't execute him. That's what he wants."

Murtagh sat down again. "That's what he wants? Explain."

"That's his motivation. He's a millenarian, a religious nut, a priest of the Second Coming and he thinks he's it. He's thirty-three, the age Jesus was when he was crucified. He must have picked this as a sure way of being executed by the state."

"A nut," Garcia said. "A religious fanatic."

"True-tell will get it out of him, and you ought to be able to get an order. You can put him in a nuthouse and throw away the key," I said.

"Huh," barked Murtagh. "Coming, Garcia?"

"I'll just be a moment," she said.

Murtagh stepped outside.

"You're not a religious fanatic," she said.

"There are possibilities in the genes, not predestination," I said. "I'm not a writer or a chef either. There's more to me than my genes."

"And there's more to me than my trigger finger."

We looked at each other, a little wary, a little uncertain, but damn she was beautiful and even more than a beautiful assistant and an outer office I needed a partner. "Blessed be the trigger happy," I said, and she was in my arms.

Sometimes in this life you've just got to ask yourself: "What would Sam Spade do?"

TRADITION

There was a man called Walter who was born out of a tank. It shouldn't have been so unusual; after all, when Pyrite was settled everyone had been born out of a tank—they only sent enough people from Earth to run the equipment and get all the babies started and bring them up. They kept right on running those tanks too, until there were enough grown-up people to have babies of their own, people to populate Pyrite City and Great Canyon and Simbardo and clear out to Fool's Gold, people enough to be talking about building cities off on the other side of the Bumpy Mountains.

By the time Walter was born they were only running the tanks if the children of the children of the first tank children didn't have enough children. There would be numbers in the news on Landing Day every year, how many babies had been born, and if it wasn't enough, how many tank babies would be born to make up. So having tank babies meant people weren't doing as much as they could, and that meant that tank babies were bad, and pretty soon the whole idea of tank babies got to be embarrassing and not to be mentioned around nice people.

Walter grew up well enough in the orphanage, and qualified as an engineer. When he was twenty-four he met and married a nice girl called Maud, who was prepared to overlook his shortcomings of background because she loved him. His shortcomings weren't very obvious as shortcomings, to tell the truth. In fact he was so good-looking and smart and hardworking that when he told people he was tank born they just didn't know what to say. Maud didn't like him to tell people, though. It made her uncomfortable.

The only way his background made him really unusual was that he didn't have any family. Everyone on Pyrite had more brothers and sisters and cousins and uncles and aunts and grandmothers and grandfathers than they could really keep track of. Walter didn't have anyone, except once he'd got married he had Maud's relations, who accepted him into the connection fairly graciously, considering. Now, Maud was a Delgarno, or at least her mother was, and her father was a Li, and you'd think that would be enough relations for anyone, and that's what Maud told her daughter Arabetsy when she was getting old enough to be asking questions.

Walter's lack of family made him surprisingly fond of Maud's family traditions. He especially loved all the holidays when they'd get together in each other's house and eat. One year it was their turn to host the Landing Day dinner for the whole clan. Walter was helping Maud cook in advance, and she asked him to cut the end off the ham for her.

"How much should I cut off?" he asked.

Maud hesitated, and Walter wondered if this was something that everyone knew except tank kids. "Oh, about ten centimetres, honey," she replied.

He cut the end off in a jiffy with his monofilament saw, and as he gave the ham to his wife he asked, "Why do you do that?"

"What?" she asked, busily sticking silverburrs on sticks.

"Why do you cut the end off that way? It's good meat, it seems to me."

"Oh honey, it's just a thing you have to do with ham. I don't know why. I do it because that's what my mother showed me how to do. Maybe you ought to ask her."

At that moment, Cleo, Maud's mother, who lived in Fool's Gold and had come early for the party, came into the kitchen looking for a drink. "Do you know why you cut the end off ham?" Walter asked her.

Cleo poured herself a drink and looked down her nose at Walter. "Did you never see anyone do that before?" she asked. "Well, I suppose it isn't surprising. I don't know exactly what it's for, but that's the way my mother taught me how to do it."

The next day as they were eating their dinner, Walter remembered about the ham. He was feeling quite stubborn about it by now. He was an engineer, and it didn't make sense to him. He wasn't ashamed of having no family, and he refused to feel that way. He went up to his grandmother-in-law, Alyssanne, who had never quite approved of him, and he asked about the ham. At first she tried to put him off, but at last she admitted that she didn't know the purpose of it either. "My mother used to cut the end off, so I do it."

Now Britney, Maud's great-grandmother, wasn't at the Landing Day party. She was old and sick, on the end of her life-extension treatments, and she lived in a retirement community over at Johnson Bay. The next time Maud and Walter took the kids over to see her, Walter was glad to have something to talk to her about as she sat in her rocker staring out across the aubergine waves.

"There's something I was wondering," he said.

Britney turned her head to look at him. She was so old that she had almost no hair and her eyes were hard to see in all the wrinkles. She still had a lovely smile. "What's that, Walter?" she asked.

"When you cook a whole ham, for the Landing Day party, why do you cut the end off before cooking it? Maud said she did it because Cleo did, and Cleo said she did it because Alyssanne did, and Alyssanne said she did it because you did. I know I'm a tank kid and don't have any family traditions of my own, so I'm kind of interested in Maud's, and this seems strange because it's good meat and it doesn't make sense."

Britney rocked a moment, and then she said, "You know, I'm glad you asked me that question. I was born from a tank myself, and my whole generation, as you know. The thing is, when the ship first landed we only had what we'd brought from Earth, before we got the Mufug Plant set up, and even then, it could only make certain things, not like today. So when I was growing up, in the orphanage, and when I was first married we didn't have any dishes big enough to take a whole ham, so we used to cut the end off to fit in the dish."

And Walter laughed, and Britney smiled her sweet smile, and Maud laughed, and Arabetsy, who was the only one of the children old enough to understand, laughed until she almost fell off the balcony into the sea.

WHAT JOSEPH FELT

When you're working with wood, sometimes, you'll be planing or cutting and there'll be a snag, an unseen snag under the grain that throws you off, and a piece you had almost done will get spoilt. Between one breath and the next it'll go from something good, something beautiful and useful and what you're working on to junk, maybe a pile of splinters, or maybe something you can patch, though you know it'll never be the same.

The feeling you have when that happens, that's the feeling I had when she told me, except it was my whole life gone to splinters in an instant.

She was the only one I ever loved, and the only one I'd ever thought of loving. The future was something I was working on, something I knew the shape of. We were going to marry in the spring, and of course I hadn't touched her. If she was pregnant then—well, there were only two rational possibilities. Someone had raped her, in which case I'd have to deal with the results of that whether I married her or not, or—well, the other possibility would mean that she wasn't who I thought she was, she wasn't the girl I'd fallen in love with. The third one, the irrational one, which was what she told me, well, it was a fairy tale, a romance, something nobody could believe, not really, not when your girlfriend just comes out with it that way.

You see, she got an angel telling her she was blessed among women. I didn't get anything, except her telling me. I'm only a carpenter.

Patch it, that was my instinct, try to smooth the knot, try to hold things together, this is my *life*.

So we got married quickly and my mother nagged at me for not waiting and my friends made crude jokes and she spent all her time with her cousin Elizabeth.

Then, just before the baby was due, the Romans called a census. The worst thing about it was that my idiotic father had misunderstood the Roman tax form, and where you were supposed to put down where you were based, which was Nazareth, where I'd lived my entire life, he'd put down Bethlehem, which was where he'd come from originally. I'd tried to change it a million times, but dealing with bureaucracy means you need bribes, which I never had, so every time there was a census, about every ten years, I had to go off to Bethlehem and go through the same stupid ritual about how no, I didn't live there . . . you can imagine. It wasn't so bad when my grandparents were still alive and I had somewhere to stay.

Then she insisted on coming with me, she wasn't going to be left in Nazareth with my mother, she wouldn't stay with Elizabeth either that time, she wanted to come.

You're supposed to humour pregnant women, and I was double humouring her, because of the circumstances. I thought it was rape, and a long road to recovery, after the baby was born.

She seemed to believe what she told me, and she'd always been very sensible before.

So she got onto the donkey and we set off, barely speaking, and I walked alongside, quietly, trying to smooth everything, trying to put a patch on it, trying to be calm and rational for both of us and hold on to what we could. We could have other children later, children of mine, and I'd do what I could for this child of hers, which I truly believed wasn't of her seeking. Whatever had happened to her we could build something together, not what we would have had, but something. That's what I kept thinking, walking along in the dust and the heat, making conversation about the scenery all that weary way.

You know the rest, the inn, the manger, the shepherds, the kings, the animals talking, the angels singing.

Though if it's true he's born to be our saviour he'll have a hard block to carve, and sorrow at the end of it.

Still, what I thought when the angels were singing and the star was shining was about the way sometimes when you're carving and you hit a knot in the grain and you realize you were going to make something quite ordinary, but now there's all this extra potential, all this incredible possibility revealed. You know then you have to go carefully, because it could suddenly all fall to splinters, but there's this moment when it's all before you and you could make something, you could make anything.

So she picked him up out of the manger and everyone was crowding around in the starlight and there was the wonderful singing. I didn't say anything, I don't talk all that much actually, but she looked over the baby's head at me and that's how I felt, at that moment, that familiar sudden shock of joy.

THE NEED TO STAY THE SAME

"The Need to Stay the Same," by Si. A review by Dorui. "The Need to Stay the Same" is the latest of Si's "humans" sequence, and at eight offerings so far the world and themes are starting to feel familiar.

This is the story of a human called Bruce who comes to the city of Quingale on the cusp of autumn. Bruce, like all Si's heroines, is an outsider with a problem. Bruce's particular and specific problem is different from those in the earlier stories—what it is and how it works out is a lot of why this is in the end worth your time, and I don't want to spoil it for you. But beyond the particulars of who Bruce is and what kind of transformation it is that has brought her to Quingale, this is something we've seen before.

In a world where humans now have a kaleidoscopic variety of options as far as gender, sexuality, and bodies go, they are still bound to the physical, they still have to live in bodies. That's the joy and horror of the series, of course, the very physicality of the characters—they eat, they make love, they move from place to place all in the physical world. Si is as good as ever at describing the sensations of humanity—the changes in temperature, the tastes, the scents, even touch, the hardest to imagine of all. There's a stunning sequence here where Bruce longs to scratch her nose but is prevented by social convention, which really made me believe what it would be like to have a nose and an itch.

But while this use of physicality was revolutionary and astonishing in the justly celebrated "Birth and Death," and still exciting and fascinating in subsequent volumes, I'm getting a little tired of it. Yes, Bruce's body makes an involuntary twitch as she shivers in a cold wind—I remember the same thing happening to Lu Song in "Living Without You." Sure, the leaves that have helped trees convert sunlight to nutrients all summer are slowly drifting to the ground, and yes, it's an amazing piece of chemical and biological imagination, but it was described in "The Flowers in the Wheelbarrow." It's interesting that now the fixed genders of earlier books have ceased to be a problem, but I never really cared about that anyway. And clever as it all is, you have to admit it's a long way removed from real life.

Si's genius is in making these "humans," so different from us, so like us in some essential ways. I'm not a huge fan of the explanations of Si's weirder inventions like "photosynthesis" and "orgasm," but I do appreciate the level at which emotion is universal. There were ways in which I could identify with Bruce, in her ever-changing quest for stability. Interpersonal relationships are one of Si's true strengths, and I really do feel after reading this that it doesn't matter if it's bodies under a sheet with heat and touch and secretions, or minds longing for merger—we reach out to each other in the same ways. Bruce's impediment is not the same kind of impediment as those we suffer, but it still has emotional resonance, and I cared. I wanted

Bruce to find fulfillment, even the strange kind of fulfillment that's what's available for humanity.

Still, in the end, eight of anything is surely enough? We've been paying attention to these "humans" for a long time, it must be hours now. This is a good addition to the series, it's powerful, and Si does manage to pull some surprises here and there. But I think it's time for a new series, for Si's wild invention to bring us something else, something with characters just this great, and ideas just as alien as the concept of physical flesh, but new.

A BURDEN SHARED

Penny woke on Tuesday morning and cautiously assessed the level of pain. If she didn't move at all, there was nothing but the familiar bone-deep ache in all her joints. That wasn't so bad, nothing stabbing, nothing grinding. Penny smiled. Ann must be having a good day. Maybe even heading for another minor remission. This was much better than it had been on Saturday, when Ann's pain had woken her with a shock she had flinched against and made worse. This was nothing more than the pain she had endured Tuesdays, Thursdays, and Saturdays for the thirty years since her daughter's birth. Still smiling, Penny eased herself to sitting and reached for the cane she kept hanging on the rail that ran along the wall. Once she had it she stood, breathing deliberately, as the smile became a grimace, then walked slowly to the bathroom, where she used the rail to lower herself carefully to the toilet seat.

That evening, as Penny was lying on the daybed grading papers for her next day's classes, there was a knock at the door. She levered herself up slowly and walked towards it. Her ex-husband Noah was on the doorstep, his gleaming Viasolo parallel parked on the street. If he'd done that, and not pulled into her driveway, he must want a favour. Too bad the pain was too much for her to consider standing on the doorstep while she found out what it was. "Hi," she said, warily. "Come in."

"How are you?" he asked as he followed her into the living room. They had been divorced for more than twenty years, after a marriage of less than ten, but seeing Noah always provoked the same mixture of exasperation and weary affection. She could recall the times when catching sight of Noah had sent thrills running through her, and also the times when just hearing two words in his careful patronizing tone had made her want to kill him. Now what she felt was gratitude that he had always been there for Ann. Well, nearly always.

"I'm fine," Penny said warily, easing herself back onto the daybed. She was stiff and exhausted from the day's pain, but he knew all about that.

"Good. Good . . ." He moved books from the grey chair onto the beige one and sat on the grey one. When he had lived here, the house had been tidier. "I hate to drop this on you, Pen, but can you possibly do tomorrow?"

"Oh no," she said.

"Penny . . ." His entitlement pressed hard on the exact places where her affection had worn thin.

"No. I can't. No way." She cut him off. "You know I'm prepared to make reasonable accommodations, but not at the last minute like this. I've arranged my classes specifically, my whole schedule is set, and tomorrow I have three senior seminars, a lecture, and an important dinner meeting. And I haven't had a day free this week. Janice is in the middle of a Chrons flare, so I took that Sunday so she could preach, and yesterday—"

"I have to fly to Port Moresby," Noah interrupted. "I'm on my way to the airport now. Old Ishi has had a stroke, and Klemperer isn't coping. I have to go. Our whole Papuan capacity is collapsing. I have to be there. It could be my career, Pen." Noah leaned forward, his hands clasped together.

"Your career is not more important than my career," Penny said, firmly, though the thought of going through the eleven-hour flight from Cleveland to Port Moresby with Ann's pain was legitimately horrifying.

"I know, but this is beyond my control. Ishi might be dying." Noah's big brown eyes, so like Ann's, were fixed on Penny's.

She had always liked Ishi, Noah's senior partner. "Do give her my best when you speak to her. And Suellen too." She deliberately looked down at the icon on the app that recorded how many papers she still had to grade, to harden her heart. "But I can't take tomorrow. Ask Lionel."

"I already did. I called him. He's rehearsing all day. *Copellia.* They open on Monday." Noah shrugged.

Penny winced. She loved her son-in-law, but she wished sometimes that Ann had found a partner whose career made it possible for him to share a little more of the burden.

"If you can't do it, there's nothing else for it, Ann will just have to shoulder her own pain tomorrow," Noah said.

The words "selfish bastard" flashed through Penny's mind, but she didn't utter them. She didn't need to. Noah knew how hard Ann's pain was to bear, and he knew how much easier it was to bear someone else's pain than one's own. So he knew that he was forcing Penny to accept another day of Ann's pain, however inconvenient it was, because he knew she wouldn't put their daughter through that. One of the things that had led to the divorce was when Noah had wished aloud that pain transference had never been invented. Penny never felt like that. Bad as enduring Ann's pain could be, it was so much better to suffer it herself than to watch her daughter suffer. After all, Penny only took the pain. That was all people could do for each other. Ann still had to bear the underlying organic condition, and the eventual degeneration it would cause.

"I'll take Thursday," Noah said, into her silence. "I really can't manage tomorrow, I have to get some sleep on the flight so I can cope when I arrive. But Friday I'll be there, I'll have found my feet, it will be all right."

Penny sighed. Mentally she had already filed this with the many other arguments she had lost to Noah over the years. "Can you at least take the pain until you get on the plane?"

"I'll do that," he said. "I'll take it right now. And thanks Pen, you're the best." He tapped at the app, and the sensation as pain left her was so delightful that she almost bounced up off the bed. His face, in contrast, seemed to age a decade as the pain hit. She reached back for the cane she no longer needed, and handed it to him with a stretch that would have been impossible moments before. "Thank you," he said, pulling himself carefully up. "I have one in the car. I always keep one there."

She walked out with him. "Do you think it's a bit better today?" she asked.

He grinned through the pain. "Better than sometimes, definitely. But you know that long term it just gets worse."

Penny nodded. Wincing as he reached for it, Noah pulled his cane from his trunk, one of the high-tech lightweight models with a folding seat and a retractable snow spike. It looked as novel next to her more traditional wooden cane as his zippy Viasolo did next to her sedate Solari.

When Penny went back in, she headed for the kitchen, almost dancing down the corridor. She was hungry, as she had not been all day. Moving without care felt like a luxury. She enjoyed standing to chop vegetables, relished taking a step to the fridge for a slice of lobster with no warning stab preventing her from moving. She sang as she stir-fried, and ate sitting at the kitchen table. If she hadn't had this break from pain she'd have ordered banh-mi, and this was so much nicer. She always liked to exercise on pain-free days. There wasn't time to go to the dojo or the pool, but she did a few squats after dinner then sat at her desk to do the grading. By the time Noah was on the plane and the pain hit her once more, she was ready for bed.

She woke Wednesday morning in absolute agony, pain ripping through her stomach like the worst imaginable period cramps, combining to set all Ann's arthritic joint pain jangling. Penny blinked, and gasped aloud. When she tried to move, she could not suppress a cry. She called her daughter right away.

Ann sounded sleepy. "Mom?"

"This is really bad, sweetie. It might be some kind of warning sign. I think you should go to the doctor."

"I'm so sorry!" Penny hadn't been living with Ann's guilt for as long as Ann's pain, so she wasn't as used to it. Her daughter had been born with the joint condition, but the guilt developed as she grew, blossoming fully only in the last decade. Penny wondered sometimes what kind of mother-daughter relationship they would have without the existence of Ann's disease. They loved each other. But Ann's pain, and the question of who felt it, had always been between them, both binding them together and keeping them apart.

"I'm happy to bear it for you," Penny said, even as a new ridge of pain ripped through her stomach. "Do you have your period?"

"Not until next week, you know that," Ann said. "Why?"

"It's just that this feels a bit like cramps," Penny said, though she had never had any cramps one-tenth this bad.

"I never have cramps," Ann said. "Let me feel this."

"No, darling, you don't want to," Penny said.

"Mom, I am not a little kid any more, and you have to let me make the decisions about my pain, just the same as anything else in my life. Let me feel it, and I'll decide whether to go to the doctor."

"Just for a minute then." Penny knew her daughter was right, but it was hard to let go all the same, to know that the agony would be inflicted on her. What kind of mother would she be if it didn't hurt her as much emotionally as it relieved her physically to press the app to return her daughter's pain? She pressed it decisively, and at once the arthritic ache was gone. Once the switch had been set up it really was that easy, though setting it up was a complicated process. For an instant Penny relaxed on the bed. Then another cramp hit her. "Mom?" Ann said. "This doesn't feel any different from normal." Penny hated to hear the pain, so familiar, coming through in her daughter's voice.

"No, I guess these cramps are something else. Maybe Janice— though it doesn't feel like that. And she's considerate. She always calls."

"Or something of your own," Ann said.

Penny laughed. The laughter hurt her stomach, so she stopped. "I didn't even consider that possibility. I'm never ill. Maybe it's some kind of menopause thing. I must be getting to that kind of age. Though I hadn't heard it feels like this."

"Go to the doctor, Mom," Ann said.

"I can't today, I'm teaching, and it's my really full day. I'll make an appointment for tomorrow." Penny stood up and walked towards the bathroom, taking the cane with her, because she'd need it soon enough, but swinging it like a baton.

"How come you had my pain if you're teaching?" Ann asked. "Did Dad duck out of it again?"

"Didn't Lionel tell you?" Penny asked, stepping under the shower.

"Dad asked Lionel?"

"He told me he had. He said Lionel's in rehearsal for *Copellia*."

"That's true. I'm so proud of him, Mom. This could be his big break, getting out of the corps, soloing. But he should have told me Dad called. I can cope with my own pain."

"Sweetie—"

"Mom." Ann's voice was firm.

"But truly, it's easier for me than it is for you." The shower cycled to hot air. "There have been studies and everything."

"Not when you have your own pain too," Ann said. "Maybe you should give me that!" Ann sounded enthusiastic.

"What, I take yours and you take mine?" Penny joked, making her way back to the bedroom.

"No, seriously, Mom! I never get to do anything for you, because you never have any pain. But now I could! And you always say how much easier it is to bear somebody else's pain. Everyone says that. Let me!"

"I'll need it to show the doctor," Penny said, pausing in pulling on her underwear and doubling up in pain as another cramp rocked her. "It wasn't too bad in the shower, but now it's biting again."

"You said you were going to the doctor tomorrow, Mom. And

if you have a full load teaching today, I should keep mine and yours!"

"No. That's not happening. I've taught with yours before. I'm used to it. But if you really want to try trading, we could do that." Penny pulled on a freshly printed academic robe.

"Fantastic!" Ann's voice was bouncy. "Let's switch, then."

Penny hadn't traded her own pain since they had tested the app with a needle jab. Unlike accepting and returning other people's pain, which she had set as shortcuts, she had to go through several layers of menu. "Accept, accept, accept," she heard Ann say, and as the cramps left her, Ann's familiar grinding joint pain came back. She sat down fast on the edge of the bed.

"Oh, Mom," Ann said, her voice full of concern. "Mom, I think you should go to the doctor now. Really. I don't think this should wait until tomorrow."

"Really?" Penny was surprised at the concern in Ann's voice.

"Really. I'm happy to bear this for you, but what even is it? I'm worried. I'm making an appointment for you right now!" This was Ann's lawyer voice, solicitous but with a competence and decisiveness she showed her clients but seldom her family. "There, she'll see you at eleven-thirty."

"Give me my pain back, then, if I'm going to the doctor," Penny said.

"No. I'll drive over and we can go to the doctor together. I'm in court this afternoon, but this morning I'm working from home."

"Pick me up from campus then. I'll take my first seminar and cancel the next. As long as I'm back by two for my lecture—is that when you're due in court?"

As Penny drove her little Solari through the crisp fall morning, she tried to think what had been so different about her conversation with Ann. It had been like dealing with a friend, an equal. Maybe Ann was finally grown up enough that they could have a new kind of relationship? Or maybe it was having pain of her own to share. Apart from the usual array of viruses and skinned knees, all the pain Penny had ever experienced had been vicarious. It was hard to imagine that in the old days she'd barely have known what pain was, and been forced to endure the sight of other people suffering without being able to help at all.

In the ten o'clock seminar, the students were each giving five-minute presentations. The third student, Regina, was hit with pain and collapsed in the middle of hers. "Duleep!" she gasped.

The other students gasped too. "Lucky Reggie!" Danee observed. "I've been signed up for Duleep for two years, but never felt it."

"While I'm sympathetic to your pain issue, let's focus on our presentations now," Penny said. "Could you continue until Regina is feeling better, Kim?"

Even hopelessly out-of-date Penny knew that Duleep was a Bollywood superstar who suffered from a kind of ulcer caused by the parasites endemic in the part of India where he had grown up. His pain was shared by his millions of fans worldwide. As with other celebrity figures who shared their pain, the recipients were thrilled to feel it. Regina's writhings seemed exaggerated to Penny, but they wore off before she felt it necessary to comment. Once restored to her normal status, Regina sat quietly listening, and redid her presentation at the end. As class ended, all the other students were crowding around to compliment her on her luck and stoicism. Penny left them to it and walked out the long way around, down the slope of the hill avoiding the steps. Ann was waiting in the plaid Honda Sky she shared with Lionel.

When she slid in, Penny was horrified to see how drawn her daughter's face was. "I'm glad we're going to the doctor with this, because the sooner it's fixed, the better," Ann said, switching the car to self-drive mode. "I don't know what this is, but it's not good, Mom." She hugged Penny, who hugged her back.

Once her blood had been drawn and tested, the diagnosis was almost instant. The doctor frowned, and ran it again, then handed the paper to Penny. "There's no easy way to tell you this," the doctor said.

"How can I be riddled with inoperable cancer?" she asked the doctor. "I didn't feel a thing until today!"

The doctor frowned. "Have you been experiencing a lot of pain?" she asked. "Sometimes that can mask symptoms."

She handed Ann the prognosis when she got back into the car. Ann hugged her again, then insisted on taking Penny's pain back before they drove away. A chilly wind was blowing the leaves from the trees at the roadside. Before there were new green leaves, Penny would be dead. She couldn't quite take it in.

"The first thing we need to do is sort out a pain management regime," Ann said. "You've helped enough people. Lots of them will be happy to help you."

"There are also painkillers, for cases like this," Penny said.

Ann flinched as if her mother had said one of the five words you don't say in church. "Mom. I love you. Other people love you. It won't come to that. You don't have to poison your body with those things, even if you are going to d-die."

"This reminds me of the time when we had your diagnosis," Penny said. "You were just a tiny baby. And you had this incurable disease that was going to give you pain forever. And your father and I were sure we could manage it. Delighted we lived now so that we could share the burden instead of being helpless and leaving you to suffer it alone." They drove on, past the college, where Penny would not now teach out the school year. "How are you going to manage, Ann?"

"I'll cope," Ann said, stalwartly. "Dad will be there. And Lionel will do what he can. I'll find a way to manage. Don't worry about me now, Mom. Think about yourself."

Penny looked out of the car window, as helpless in the face of her daughter's suffering as any parent had ever been.

THREE SHOUTS
ON A HILL

Dramatis Personae
(in order of appearance)

TUREEN, an Irish lord
BRIAN, his son
KEVIN, his son
AIDEEN, his daughter

LUGH, the king of Ireland
DANU, his wife and advisor

A DRAGON

AN AFRICAN GATEKEEPER
THE KING OF THE AFRICANS

THE MASTER OF THE WALLS
THE KING OF THE INCAS

THE QUEEN OF THE INCAS

An American **GRANDMOTHER**

A Japanese **GATEKEEPER**
A Japanese **CAT**
THE EMPEROR OF JAPAN

THE QUEEN OF THE CATS

THE POPE

OLIVER CROMWELL
KING ARTHUR

ACT I

DANU: A blessing on all those who hear this story, and a blessing on all those who tell it.

Scene 1: Tureen's Hall. TUREEN is sitting cleaning a gun. Enter BRIAN, KEVIN, and AIDEEN.

TUREEN: Call yourself children of mine! The way you three come slinking into the house shamefaced under cover of darkness you'd think you'd committed murder.

BRIAN: Sorry, Father . . .

TUREEN: You have? Well, I hope it was nobody important!

KEVIN: Actually . . .

TUREEN: Well then I hope at least you've managed to hide the body!

AIDEEN: Oh yes, Father, we have hidden the body! We've hidden it so well it'll never be found.

TUREEN: Where have you hidden it?

KEVIN: It was like this, Father, we were walking along the road coming back from Tara and this stranger challenged—

TUREEN: I didn't ask for justifications, I asked where you hid the body.

AIDEEN: We buried it at the crossroads where the road from Tara crosses the road from Galway and we planted some fast-growing willow above it. In a few days nobody will know the earth's been disturbed.

TUREEN: There are better things you might have contrived, but that's not bad.

KEVIN: It was Aideen's idea.

BRIAN: He was so astonishingly rude—

TUREEN: By the fact you admitted to murder and by the fact there are three of you and only one of him, there's nothing you can say that will justify yourselves to me. If you weren't my own children, I'd want nothing to do with any of you.

BRIAN: Sorry, Father.

KEVIN: But—Sorry, Father. It was thoughtless of us.

TUREEN: Thoughtless!

AIDEEN: You haven't yet asked us who he was.

TUREEN: Who was he, then? I'm not sure I want to know.

AIDEEN: We didn't know until too late. We thought he was just some incredibly rude old man. But after he was dead, we found out. He was Kian.

TUREEN: Kian? Kian, the son of Danka? Kian the father of the new king?

BRIAN: Sorry, Father.

TUREEN [shocked]: Well.
   Well, that's a bad business.

That's about as bad as it can be.
   If Lugh finds out your lives won't be worth an apple core.

BRIAN: Sorry, Father.

TUREEN: It's not me you should apologise to.

AIDEEN: Nobody will find the body. King Lugh will never know.

TUREEN [*cheering up a little*]: On the other hand, you know, he just might take compensation.

AIDEEN: He's Lugh of the Cunning Hand, the greatest of all heroes. He's the greatest warrior and the greatest wizard and the greatest craftsman in all Ireland. He's newly appointed king, to lead us against Cromwell when he comes back. Why would he take compensation from us when we've killed his father?

TUREEN: Kian was a cantankarous old cuss.

KEVIN: He came up and asked us to give way. Demanded it. We'd have given way at once if—

TUREEN: On the other hand, there were three of you, and you're all well-armed young folk in the prime of life. Kian was an old man, alone.

KEVIN: He drew his sword first.

TUREEN: But then again, Lugh was brought up by his mother.

BRIAN: That's old news.

TUREEN: What I mean is he didn't know his father well.

AIDEEN: That could be good or bad.

KEVIN: It's bad. If he'd known him well he'd understand why anybody might just naturally kill him after he picked a fight with them as they were coming home along the road peacefully. It's a notable wonder that man lived to be old.

TUREEN: All considered, I think you should offer compensation. Lugh will set it high, since Kian was his father, but not higher than we can pay, since Kian started it. He knew him well enough to know that was likely. And he needs us. Cromwell is coming back. Last time, Cromwell killed everybody in Ireland except seven pregnant women who hid in a cave, my mother among them. Lugh can't afford to waste his best warriors and wizards at a time like this.

AIDEEN: We hid the body.

TUREEN: Well, I admit that does look bad.

AIDEEN: Only if he finds it. And he'll never find it. And if he did find it, who's to say who killed him? Nobody was there. If none of the four of us speaks of it, nobody will ever know.

BRIAN: If we went to him, Lugh could ask our lives. Kian was his father, after all.

TUREEN: Lugh is a proud man, but a fair one. He'll be a good king. He's just the man we need to lead us against Cromwell. I think you should throw yourselves on his mercy. But—

AIDEEN: Nobody will find the body. Willow grows fast.

Scene 2: Lugh's Hall, 3 months later. LUGH and DANU are sitting on the seat of judgement, AIDEEN, BRIAN, and KEVIN are standing before them.

LUGH: You know why I have called you here.

AIDEEN: No, lord. Is Cromwell coming early?

LUGH: My grandfather has not changed the date appointed for our meeting.

DANU: Can't you guess any reason why the king might have summoned the three of you?

AIDEEN: No, lady, tell us.

DANU: There was a minstrel here last night.

KEVIN: A minstrel?

LUGH: A minstrel with a harp of willow, willow that she found growing at the crossroads. Ever since the minstrel made the harp, that harp would only play one tune, and the words of that tune were this: "The children of Tureen have killed the father of the king."

KEVIN: What a tedious harp.

LUGH: You killed my father and now you're joking about it? I should nail your guts to a tree and have you lashed around the tree until your guts are all pulled out and tripping you. I should have you flayed and wear your skin for my cloak. I should—

BRIAN: I'm sorry, lord! I'm so sorry.

AIDEEN: Will you take compensation?

LUGH: Compensation? For the murder of my father? From the people who killed my father and concealed his body so that the willow wands of the harp had to call out to me for vengeance?

KEVIN: I told you he wouldn't take it.

AIDEEN: We did kill him. And we were three against one, and he was an old man. But Kian provoked us. He was a provoking man. He demanded we fight him, or we'd never have drawn our weapons. We're loyal to you and our father is loyal to you, and we shouldn't be fighting among ourselves when Cromwell is coming.

DANU: Perhaps you should have thought of that before you fought with Kian. Nevertheless, my lord, I think you should set compensation.

LUGH: What? *[Danu whispers in his ear.]*

AIDEEN *[to her brothers]*: I think we're saved!

LUGH: I will take compensation. And the compensation will be this. Three apples, and a gun, and a chariot with two horses, and a black cloak, and a gold cup, and a clockwork toy, and a feather, and three shouts on a hill. If you think that is too much, tell me now, and I will remit part of it, because I will never remit a hair of it once we have agreed. Give me your pledge before what you hold holy that you will pay it, and I will give you my pledge that I will ask no more.

KEVIN: A feather?

AIDEEN: We will pay it, by all the gods, we would pay it a hundred times over.

KEVIN: We will gladly pay what you ask, by the beard of my father.

BRIAN: Oh yes, by father, son, and holy ghost, and so, so, sorry.

LUGH: Well . . .

The three apples are three golden apples from the Garden of the Hesperides at the bottom of the sea. They are guarded by a dragon. They are the size of the head of a child, they do not diminish when they are eaten, they come back to the hand when they are thrown, and they heal wounds and cure ailments. I will accept no other apples but these three apples.

And the gun that you have agreed to give me is the cannon that belongs to the pope of Rome, that's mounted on the walls of his city and that protects it from all enemies. That gun can slay a thousand armed men with one shot. It's defended by all the guards of Switzerland.

DANU: It'll be very useful to us in our fight against Cromwell.

AIDEEN: I can see that. Go on, let us know what else it is we have to bring.

KEVIN: I'm very curious about that feather.

LUGH: You're not cowards at least.

BRIAN: Oh no, lord!

LUGH: Well, the chariot with two horses belongs to the king of the Africans. The horses can run on land or water, and they're the fastest horses that were ever seen, they can go in an eyeblink from one end of Ireland to the other.

The black cloak belongs to the king of the cats. Anyone who wears it can go unseen and unheard, and the only way you would know they were there was by smelling them.

AIDEEN: I understand, go on please.

LUGH: The gold cup belongs to the king of the Incas. If water is poured from it onto any dead person they will return to life the next morning. They have all their strength, and are as they were in life, except that they cannot speak.

DANU: You see how helpful that could be in battle.

KEVIN: Only if it's a long battle.

LUGH: The last battle against Cromwell lasted seven days and nights.

KEVIN: Yes, it would certainly be useful in that situation.

LUGH: The clockwork toy belongs to the emperor of Japan. It's thirty feet tall and ten men can ride on it. The sound of its voice sends enemies running, and its feet can crush a man in full armour.

BRIAN: Cromwell will flee from Ireland like a whipped cur!

KEVIN: Hush, now we're getting to the feather.

LUGH: Ah yes, the feather. The feather belongs to the king of the Americans. It is the greatest treasure in their land. When it is stroked one way, it summons the thunder, and when it is stroked the other it summons the lightning.

KEVIN: That's a feather worth questing for.

AIDEEN: And the three shouts on the hill?

LUGH: You think you will achieve the other things with no trouble?

AIDEEN: I just want to know the full measure of what we have already promised.

LUGH: Those three shouts you shall give on the hill of Glaston-bury, where King Arthur lies sleeping, and where all of the armies of the English have sworn no sound shall be made that might disturb his sleep. Besides that, my father Kian was fostered among them, and learned arms there, so even if I forgive you, his English friends will not.

DANU: Do this last. And before you do it, bring the other things you have gathered to us, so that they will not be lost when—if you fall.

AIDEEN: Well, it's a hard task you set us, but we shall do our best.

Scene 3: Tureen's hall. Present are TUREEN, AIDEEN, BRIAN, and KEVIN.

KEVIN: And if you stroke it the other way it brings the lightning. Then we have to return with all of that and give three shouts on the hill of Glastonbury.

TUREEN: Well, that's bad, that is.

AIDEEN: I'm trying to decide the best order of doing it. Some of the things would help us a great deal in getting some of the others.

BRIAN: The apples would be useful if we were hurt. Or the cup if we happened to be killed.

TUREEN: You might be killed ten times over before bringing all these treasures back to Ireland.

BRIAN: The cloak might let us sneak in and take things. Or the cannon would be useful in killing the owners of some of the other treasures.

KEVIN: Don't worry, brother, we'll have our swords and spears if it comes to that.

AIDEEN: The chariot would make it much more convenient for going about the place—it's a long way to Rome, never mind Japan, the kingdom of the Incas, and the kingdom of the Americans. But how would we get to Africa?

TUREEN: You should borrow Mananan's boat. That boat can find its own way if you ask it where to go. It can go above the sea or under the sea.

KEVIN: But why would he lend it to us?

TUREEN: Mananan has a gesa that he can never refuse the second thing asked of him on any day. So you should go and ask to borrow his horse, and when he refuses, ask to borrow his boat. He'll let you have it for a day, which should be long enough to go to the bottom of the sea and get the apples and then go to Africa and get the chariot. Once you have the chariot you can give back the boat and go about freely.

AIDEEN: Thank you, Father, that's good advice.

TUREEN: But make sure you have the boat back on time, or Mananan will be after you, and he's a very bad man to anger, besides being a neighbour of mine.

✯ ✯ ✯

Act II

Scene 1: In Mananan's boat, directly above the Garden of Hesperides, in the sea near the island of Skye

AIDEEN: I've made three magic sticks that will let us breathe underwater. The only problem is that they'll only last for an hour, so we want to be in and out as quickly as possible.

KEVIN: Do you think we can fight a dragon in an hour?

AIDEEN: Maybe we won't have to fight.

KEVIN: Oh, so he'll just give us the apples?

AIDEEN: Maybe we can trick the dragon.

BRIAN: How would we trick a dragon?

AIDEEN: I'll think of something. Just follow my lead.

BRIAN: All right then.

KEVIN: Should we break the sticks?

AIDEEN: Yes, just like any magic sticks, crack them down hard on any part of your body.

BRIAN: Ow.

KEVIN: Let's get down then. [*The boat descends.*]

AIDEEN: It's very pretty underwater.

KEVIN: I see apple trees, that must be the garden.

AIDEEN: Let's go down inside—the walls are only at the sides. Maybe we can—

DRAGON: Greetings, mortals from the world of air.

AIDEEN: Greetings, Sir Dragon, the most magnificent, the most splendid, the most terrifying, the supreme. So wonderful a dragon are you that as you curled around these underwater apple trees we thought you were a great wall.

DRAGON: Enough politeness. Introduce yourselves properly.

AIDEEN: I am Aideen, the daughter of Tureen, and these are my brothers Kevin and Brian.

DRAGON: Irish, are you?

AIDEEN: Yes, honoured dragon.

DRAGON: Not Greek?

AIDEEN: Not at all Greek.

DRAGON: Good, because I don't like Greeks. There was a Greek fellow once who came here and stole my apples.

KEVIN: Then we're too late?

DRAGON: What do you mean, too late?

AIDEEN: My brothers and I came hoping to see the famous golden apples of the Hesperides. It would be very sad if some Greek had come and stolen them.

DRAGON: Well, he stole some. Apples grow on trees, you know. They've grown back.

KEVIN: Well, that's good news. I see them now. Amazing. More the size of grapefruit than apples.

DRAGON: You haven't come to steal them yourselves?

AIDEEN: No, oh no. We came to see them, and of course to see the famous dragon.

DRAGON: Famous, am I?

AIDEEN: Famous guardian of the famous apples. There's a poem about you.

DRAGON: A poem? Interesting. But you needn't think I'll go to sleep while you recite it to me. That Greek fellow got away with that, but I'm wary now.

AIDEEN: Shall I recite it, while you listen alertly?

DRAGON: I suppose you might as well. One likes to know what people are saying about one, after all.

AIDEEN: King of apples, king of the sea
  Pearl, light green filtered,
  Under.
  Floating, sinking, stretching,
  Drawing down.
  There will be bone,
  There will be twisted shell,
  And they will be the same.
  There will be eyes and arms,
  Opening, reaching,
  There, under,
  In the lacy light
  In the afternoon,
  Settling slow to the seabed
  With fishes swimming in and out
  And the apple trees
  Impossible, undersea, blossoming slow
  Without breath,
  Drifting, opening
  Settling
  Under
  Drawing down
  Under
  Reaching, reaching,
  Opening,

Golden scales falling,
Arms embracing
That will be pale coral, spiralled shell
Old bones to new rock . . .

DRAGON: I'm not asleep! I see you two sneaking around behind me while your sister lulls me. Tries to lull me. That was the worst poem I ever heard. Oh, draw your sword will you?

KEVIN: I knew it wouldn't work, but take this!

DRAGON: Did nobody tell you it's cheating to go in under the arm that way?

AIDEEN: Brian, quick, get the apples!

BRIAN: I've got them.

KEVIN: He's dead, I think. Fortunately, fire doesn't work too well underwater.

AIDEEN: Well struck, brother.

BRIAN: Boat, take us back up, quickly.

KEVIN: That was a very strange poem. I thought our air was going to run out while you were going on and on. Under. What did you mean, repeating under over and over like that?

BRIAN: She was trying to bore him to sleep.

AIDEEN: It's a pity. If I'd known what the blood would look like billowing out red in the green water I'd have put that in too.

Scene 2: On the coast of Africa

KEVIN: I hope you have a better plan for getting the chariot from the king of the Africans.

AIDEEN: Why? That worked pretty well.

KEVIN: Only because I was ready.

BRIAN: Only because you saw the soft spot when the dragon turned around listening to the poem.

AIDEEN: We don't have to worry about being wounded. The apples will cure us. And if we throw them, they'll come back to us, and they're huge, so they seem as if they'd do some damage. We should take one each and bear that in mind.

KEVIN: How are we going to get in? We're going to be really conspicuous. I haven't seen a single other white person since we got here.

AIDEEN: We'll tell them we're poets come all the way from Ireland.

BRIAN: Not everyone is as vain or as stupid as that dragon.

KEVIN: Not everybody is as slow and stupid as you.

BRIAN: I got the apples, didn't I?

KEVIN: Eventually.

AIDEEN: Come on. Mananan will be angry with Father if we don't get the boat back soon.

GATEKEEPER: Who goes there?

AIDEEN: I am Aideen, a poet from Ireland come to perform before the king of the Africans. These are my brothers Kevin and Brian.

GATEKEEPER: I'm afraid you've been misinformed.

AIDEEN: In what respect?

GATEKEEPER: Africa is a continent containing an empire, several kingdoms, and an oligarchy, divided by diverse deserts, jungles, and mountainous regions, inhabited by various populations who arrange their own political affairs. It is much bigger than Europe. It does not have a single king, any more than there's a single king of the Europeans.

BRIAN: There isn't?

AIDEEN: My magic boat (I have a magic boat you see, like most well-known Irish poets) brought me here when I asked for the king of the Africans. So the king of this place must be the best-known king of Africa, or the greatest king.

GATEKEEPER: The best known to Irish magic boats in any case. Did you come all this way alone, just the three of you?

BRIAN: We're heroes. Who else would we need?

GATEKEEPER: I don't suppose you'd like to leave your weapons here?

KEVIN: No, we like to keep them with us.

GATEKEEPER: I thought as much. Well, I'm sure the king will welcome you. Irish poets are certainly a novelty at court. Come in.

KEVIN: This isn't going to work.

GATEKEEPER: Your Majesty, allow me to present the Irish poet Aideen, and her brothers Kevin and Brian.

AIDEEN: We heard of the fame of your court and wanted to recite before you.

GATEKEEPER: They also have a magic boat.

KING OF THE AFRICANS: A magic boat, eh? Perhaps you should check that out, Gatekeeper, while they recite for me.

GATEKEEPER: I'm ahead of you.

AIDEEN: Brian . . .

BRIAN: What?

AIDEEN: Kevin?

KEVIN: I'll go with you, Sir Gatekeeper, and show you our boat.

GATEKEEPER: Maybe later.

KING OF THE AFRICANS: The thing is, I have a magic chariot.

AIDEEN: Good heavens. What can it do?

KING OF THE AFRICANS: It can run on either the land or the water, and it can get you from one end of Africa to the other in an hour and a half.

BRIAN: I heard—

KEVIN: Africa is a lot bigger than Ireland.

AIDEEN: Our boat can only go on the sea, but it can take you anywhere you ask to go, and it's also very fast. Perhaps we could have a race?

GATEKEEPER: An excellent idea, don't you think, Your Majesty?

KING OF THE AFRICANS: An excellent idea. Let's go down to the shore. Gatekeeper, saddle the horses.

AIDEEN: Perhaps, to make it more interesting, you should take the boat and I should take the chariot.

KING OF THE AFRICANS: I'm not sure my magic horses would perform as well for anyone else.

AIDEEN: You have magic horses too?

KING OF THE AFRICANS: They're a set.

AIDEEN: How many can your chariot hold?

KING OF THE AFRICANS: Three . . . maybe four.

AIDEEN: Then how about if I ride with you, and your gatekeeper rides with my brothers? My boat can also hold four.

KING OF THE AFRICANS: It sounds like an excellent boat.

AIDEEN: It is. And your chariot sounds excellent too.

KING OF THE AFRICANS: Can your boat go up waterfalls? We have a number of notable waterfalls in our country that I often take my chariot up.

AIDEEN: I've never tried. It can go down to the bottom of the sea.

KING OF THE AFRICANS: And how do you breathe there?

KEVIN: That takes separate magic.

BRIAN: It's a stick, you break it on yourself.

KEVIN: After that you can breathe underwater.

BRIAN: But it only lasts an hour.

KING OF THE AFRICANS: A very useful sort of magic. I don't suppose you would consider relocating? We could use another wizard, and another two warriors would also be sure to come in handy. I'm considering conquering Egypt soon.

AIDEEN: It's very tempting, but there's to be a war in Ireland and we'll be needed to defend our home and our old father. Besides, I'm not a wizard, I'm just a poet who happens to know a little magic. And the magic I know isn't very useful in battle. But if you'd like to breathe underwater, I can give you this stick. Let's race out to that island out there in the distance, and when we get there, break it on yourself and dive into the water.

KING OF THE AFRICANS: Yes! Wonderful! I've always wanted to breathe underwater.

GATEKEEPER: Wait. No. That would leave her alone in your chariot.

KEVIN: Well, it was worth a try.

AIDEEN: Let's race.

GATEKEEPER: And they're off. The boat pulls ahead at first, but as Madagascar gets closer the chariot is coming up fast on the inside. Can they do it? Can they do it? Kevin's getting the last ounce of speed out of the boat, he clearly knows just how to handle it, but the chariot is pulling into the lead. But wait! What's this? We agreed that Aideen wouldn't use her magic water-breathing stick, but she's getting a stick out and breaking it over the king. She's grabbing the reins. Watch out, Your Majesty! Watch—(glub)

BRIAN: You didn't need to throw him overboard.

KEVIN: I was getting sick of him rattling on that way. You'd think we couldn't see what was happening.

BRIAN: I hope he can swim.

KEVIN: Hey, Aideen, good work getting the chariot!

AIDEEN: I feel a bit bad about it.

KEVIN: Why?

AIDEEN: He wanted to breathe underwater, and I didn't have any of those sticks left. So I turned him into a dolphin.

BRIAN: But don't dolphins have to come up to breathe?

AIDEEN: Yes. That's why I feel a bit bad. Where's the gatekeeper?

KEVIN: Swimming to Madagascar.

Scene 3: Tureen's Hall

TUREEN: Have you returned Mananan's boat?

KEVIN: Yes, back where it belongs.

TUREEN: In good condition, I hope? I like to be on good terms with my neighbours—when my children aren't murdering them that is.

AIDEEN: He's not pleased that we tricked him into borrowing it, but we didn't do it any harm. It was very useful. Father—do you think we should give Lugh the apples now?

BRIAN: We should keep them. That way if we get hurt we can heal quickly.

KEVIN: We haven't got hurt yet.

BRIAN: All the more reason to hold on to them.

AIDEEN: Also, I need to borrow a map. We didn't need one before, because Mananan's boat knows the way, but you have to guide the chariot.

TUREEN: Have you murdered anybody else while you were away?

KEVIN: No! Well, I killed a dragon.

TUREEN: Dragons don't count. You didn't kill the African king?

AIDEEN: I turned him into a dolphin.

BRIAN: There was his gatekeeper.

KEVIN: It wasn't all that far to shore.

TUREEN: The last time you tried to keep something from Lugh it went very badly. He's bound to find out from Mananan that you were here. I'd take him the apples if I were you.

AIDEEN: That's what I thought.

KEVIN: What if he wants the chariot too?

AIDEEN: He must know that we need it to have any chance of getting him the things before Cromwell arrives.

KEVIN: He might not worry about that. He's destined to kill Cromwell.

BRIAN: Destiny isn't so simple.

AIDEEN: Brian's right. And besides, killing Cromwell isn't winning the battle. If he kills Cromwell and everybody's dead except seven pregnant women in a cave—

TUREEN: Like last time . . .

AIDEEN: —Like last time, you can't exactly call that winning.

TUREEN: Don't forget the map.

Scene 4: Lugh's Hall

AIDEEN: We have the apples, and we're delivering them to you now.

LUGH: Good. Though three apples isn't much for the life of my own father.

AIDEEN: We'll get the other things. We just wanted you to have the apples now in case.

LUGH: Haven't you got anything else?

AIDEEN: We have the chariot. But we need it to get to all the places we need to go.

DANU: She has a point there, beloved. If they're going to go to South America, and North America, and Japan—

LUGH: All right, keep the chariot for now. But don't think I've forgotten what you've done! At the end of all this, you'll still have to give three shouts on a hill.

KEVIN: What will we shout, I wonder?

Act III

Scene 1: In the Kingdom of the Incas, the Children of Tureen are walking through a city marked on their map as El Dorado.

BRIAN: Is this city really made of solid gold?

AIDEEN: I expect it's just gold plated. It certainly is flashy when the sun strikes it.

KEVIN: With all this gold, I expect they wouldn't miss one golden cup. We could just ask for it and go.

AIDEEN: I doubt golden cups that can bring people back to life are any more common here than they would be most places. It's probably just made of gold because they have lots of gold. If we made a magic cup we'd make it out of something we have plenty of in Ireland. Wood, like my magic sticks.

BRIAN: Rain, maybe.

KEVIN: The problem will be telling it from all the others. In most king's halls, a golden cup would stand out. Here, they could hide it in plain sight.

BRIAN: What are we going to say?

AIDEEN: The poet trick seems to be working.

KEVIN: I wouldn't call that working!

BRIAN: What are those weird animals?

AIDEEN: Leave them alone, they're not important.

BRIAN: That one spat at me!

KEVIN: She told you to leave them alone.

MASTER OF THE WALLS: I am the master of the walls. What brings you to the hidden city of Machu Picchu?

BRIAN: I thought it was called El Dorado.

MASTER: That is what the Spaniards call it.

AIDEEN: I am Aideen, the daughter of Tureen, a poet from Ireland. These are my brothers, Kevin and Brian.

BRIAN: Why do you always mention Kevin first?

KEVIN: Because I'm older. Or maybe because you're covered in spit from that disgusting goat-thing.

MASTER: That's a llama.

KEVIN: Thank you, that disgusting llama.

MASTER: I'm pleased to meet you all, but what brings you here?

AIDEEN: I wanted to perform poetry before the king of the Incas.

MASTER: Interesting. And how did you find us?

AIDEEN: The city is marked on my father's map.

MASTER: And where did your father get that map?

AIDEEN: I don't know. Ireland?

MASTER: Will you leave your weapons here?

KEVIN: We'd rather keep them, thank you.

MASTER: Well, you'd better come and perform your poetry. The king isn't very fond of poetry, as he's only six years old, but the queen might like it.

AIDEEN: I could manage a nursery rhyme.

MASTER: Queen of the Incas, young King of the Incas, I have here the children of Tureen, come from Ireland to perform poetry for you.

KING OF THE INCAS: Go on then.

QUEEN OF THE INCAS: Yes, relieve our boredom with some verse.

KEVIN: Every cup in this room is gold. I knew it.

AIDEEN: The sun rises on the golden splendor,

The sun sets in the evening,
Greatest treasure of the Incas is gold,
Where is the magical cup of renewal?
Who can say where it is?

BRIAN: That's even worse than last time.

QUEEN OF THE INCAS: Is that it?

KING OF THE INCAS: That was really boring. Can we kill them now?

QUEEN OF THE INCAS: And it had a certain thematic issue that worries me.

MASTER: Yes, it seemed worryingly concerned with our greatest treasure.

AIDEEN: My father doesn't believe there's any such cup.

BRIAN: What?

AIDEEN: My father, who makes maps with your secret cities marked on them, doesn't believe you have a magic cup. We came here because we wanted to see it. If it even exists.

QUEEN OF THE INCAS: It certainly exists.

KING OF THE INCAS: Can we put them to death yet, Mother? They have come to the secret city uninvited. And they have a forbidden map!

AIDEEN: If the cup exists, let me see it.

QUEEN OF THE INCAS: The master of the walls keeps it.

KING OF THE INCAS: Kill them, kill them already! Guards!

MASTER: Should I show them the cup first, my king?

KING OF THE INCAS: All right. I'd like to see it anyway.

MASTER: Here it is.

AIDEEN: Thank you. I doubted myself. What a lot of guards you have.

MASTER: Yes, it's useful when thieves come wanting our treasure.

KEVIN: Six each, I make it!

AIDEEN: Meet you back at the chariot!

BRIAN: Father isn't going to like this. And I do wish we'd kept those magic apples.

Scene 2: America. The children of Tureen are sitting dispiritedly at the bank of the Mississippi. An American GRANDMOTHER is walking past.

KEVIN: We've been here longer than anywhere else, but so far, all we've learned about the Americans is that they don't even have a king. What kind of people don't have a king? Or a queen. Why don't they just elect one of the royal kin like we do when we don't have a king? Why, there's not a field in Ireland that doesn't have its own king.

AIDEEN: They don't think much of my poetry either.

BRIAN: That would be because it's awful.

AIDEEN: However it is, I've been going around dropping hints about feathers here and there and nobody bites.

GRANDMOTHER: Young lady, you've been talking to the men.

AIDEEN: Yes, Grandmother, because it's the men who always have the power in the lands where I come from.

KEVIN: Well—

BRIAN: That's not exactly true.

GRANDMOTHER: Here among the people of the plains the men have one kind of power and the women have another. If you want to know about magic feathers, you shouldn't be asking the men.

AIDEEN: I do want to know about magic feathers. Go away, brothers.

KEVIN: Go where?

AIDEEN: Go back to the chariot.

KEVIN: But I particularly wanted—

AIDEEN: Kevin, go back to the chariot!

BRIAN: Men in charge, I don't think.

AIDEEN: Now tell me about magic feathers, Grandmother.

GRANDMOTHER: You already know about one kind.

AIDEEN: I do? Oh, I do. Lark's feathers bound to a stick for turning into a bird.

GRANDMOTHER: I noticed the sticks you carry.

AIDEEN: I'd happily trade you any magic stick you like for a magic thunder feather.

GRANDMOTHER: What do you have?

AIDEEN: I'm out of sticks for breathing underwater, but I have two for turning into dolphins or pigs, and three each of eagle and hound.

GRANDMOTHER: A pig? Why would you want to turn into a pig?

AIDEEN: You might want to turn somebody else into a pig. My brothers, for instance.

GRANDMOTHER: I understand why you Europeans like horses, but your other animals are very strange.

AIDEEN: We're not Europeans, we're Irish.

GRANDMOTHER: It all looks the same from here. I'll trade you a thunder feather for two hounds and an eagle.

AIDEEN: Done!

GRANDMOTHER: But you have to choose it for yourself, out of this bag full of feathers, and you have to do it without touching them.

AIDEEN: What feather would call the thunder? The sky here is so high up and far away, the plains are so wide, the mountains so high. It's not like Ireland, where the sky comes down to touch the ground, all grey and misty and damp. They call my home the emerald isle because it rains every day and makes the grass green. Here everything is dry and you can see thunder coming days away. This is thunder country, while my home is a land of soft rains. At home the bird that calls the thunder is the black crow, flying on the edge of the storm, waiting for the clouds to tear open and show what lies beyond, waiting for the leven to strike and the blood to flow. But here the skies are wider, the lightning strikes fiercer, the people have no kings, and the grandmothers do the magic. I don't know what bird dropped that great red-and-black feather. It might be some kind of eagle. But that's the feather that speaks to me of your prairie storms, that's the feather of the thunder bird. I'll take that feather, Grandmother.

GRANDMOTHER: Here. Your poetry isn't as bad as everybody said.

AIDEEN: Thank you.

Scene 3: The children of Tureen are standing outside the walls of Kyoto.

AIDEEN: Kevin, you take the feather. Brian, you take the cup.

BRIAN: You're not going to pretend to be a poet again here, are you?

AIDEEN: It's a good disguise, because poets have a reason to be wandering about the world looking for patrons.

BRIAN: Well how about if I'm the poet for a change?

AIDEEN: Can you make up poems?

BRIAN: I'm as good as you are, anyway.

KEVIN: You know, Japan is a really strange country, so far away and different. What if they don't have poets?

AIDEEN: Everybody has poets, Kevin.

BRIAN: What if they don't speak Irish?

AIDEEN: Don't be silly.

GATEKEEPER: Welcome to Kyoto, ancestral home of the emperor of Japan.

KEVIN: Oh good, you speak Irish.

GATEKEEPER: Everybody speaks Irish, young man, that goes without saying.

AIDEEN: Brian!

BRIAN: Oh—yes. I am Brian, the son of Tureen, a poet from Ireland, and this is my brother Kevin and my sister Aideen.

GATEKEEPER: Please come in, and do enjoy your time in Kyoto.

BRIAN: I wonder if you'd mind telling me what kind of poetry is in fashion here.

GATEKEEPER: Oh, certainly. We're very fond of haikus, which are short poems containing seventeen syllables. The first line has five, the second seven, and the third line five syllables.

AIDEEN: Brian, stop counting on your fingers.

GATEKEEPER: They are also supposed to contain a reference to the season.

BRIAN: Thank you.

GATEKEEPER: Come in, enjoy your stay.

KEVIN: You don't seem very worried about letting three heavily armed people walk into your city.

GATEKEEPER: No, should I be? Are you planning to attack us?

KEVIN: We'd hardly say if we were.

AIDEEN: Of course we're not. My brother was just remarking on how friendly you are, compared to some places we've been, where they ask us to leave our weapons outside.

GATEKEEPER: You see, we don't have to worry about that kind of thing, because we have mechs.

KEVIN: Mechs?

GATEKEEPER: Mechs. We've always had mechs in Japan. They keep us safe from attack, so we don't have to worry about it.

AIDEEN: Are they by any chance clockwork mechanisms thirty feet tall that allow ten men to ride on them, that terrify enemies with the sound of their voice, and that can crush an armed enemy beneath their feet?

GATEKEEPER: I see their fame has spread even to the barbarian Irish.

BRIAN: Haiku are easy
  With winter come many mechs,
  Miscalculation.

GATEKEEPER: You'll get the hang of it.

AIDEEN: We had heard of your mechs, but nobody told us how many you had.

GATEKEEPER: Oh, we have lots and lots.

AIDEEN: I think my own king would really like one, back in Ireland.

GATEKEEPER: He'd better learn how to make one then. Have a nice day.

AIDEEN *[walking away]*: I don't think they'll trade us one, and I don't know how we could steal one.

KEVIN: Maybe we should go to Rome and get the gun and come back. A gun that kills a thousand people would make short work of this place.

AIDEEN: Either it would kill the mechs or it wouldn't. Either way, we wouldn't have one to take home. We need to trick them.

KEVIN: Maybe we could take a hostage and make them give us one.

AIDEEN: That might work.

BRIAN: Summer has hot days
  Japan is far from Ireland
  Disinclination.

KEVIN: Stop it!

AIDEEN: Who would make a good hostage?

KEVIN: That gatekeeper?

AIDEEN: It would be good if we could get to the emperor.

KEVIN: With Brian's poetry?

AIDEEN: It's just counting syllables, how hard can it be?

BRIAN: Cat on the doorstep
  I wonder where their king lives
  Constantinople?

KEVIN: You didn't mention the seasons.

AIDEEN: I wonder where their king does live.

KEVIN: Father will know.

AIDEEN: I don't want to go home and leave the things we've got already when they could turn out to be useful. Cat, where does your king live?

CAT: Why should I tell you?

KEVIN: Typical cat.

AIDEEN: We could—

KEVIN: What, bring it back to life? Call the thunder for it?

CAT: Cats have nine lives, we don't need more. And why would we want thunder?

AIDEEN: Why would anyone? I was going to say we could give you a fish.

CAT: Have you got a fish?

AIDEEN: We could get one.

CAT: Get one, then we'll talk.

KEVIN: Cats are just so smug.

AIDEEN: Are these houses made of paper?

KEVIN: No, surely not, paper would burn too easily.

AIDEEN: It is paper. How unusual.

BRIAN: I saw a cat but
    I haven't seen any mechs
    Winterization.

KEVIN: I don't think the last line has to be all one word.

AIDEEN: He's right.

KEVIN: Winterization?

AIDEEN: I haven't seen any mechs either. I wonder where they are.

KEVIN: They'd probably come running if we drew our swords.

AIDEEN: I wonder.

KEVIN: That looks like a palace over there.

BRIAN: Spring—

KEVIN: Shut up. I've had about enough of that. We're going to die when we give the three shouts on the hill, and I can't be any more dead for fratricide.

AIDEEN: We could bring you back to life with the cup and kill you again.

KEVIN: We could do that with Brian. Then he wouldn't be able to talk, which would be a big improvement.

BRIAN: Sorry, sorry! I was just trying to practice.

[Enter the emperor of Japan and some members of his court.]

AIDEEN: Excuse me, are you the emperor of Japan?

EMPEROR: I am. Kindly remove your sword from my neck.

AIDEEN: I shall do so as soon as you give me a mech, which I promise I shall take home to Ireland and never return to Japan.

EMPEROR: Have you not heard of the power of my mighty mechs? They will slay you.

AIDEEN: Not before I cut your throat. And you will observe that my brothers have also drawn their swords and are threatening the lives of two of your companions.

EMPEROR: Give you a mech?

AIDEEN: Yes, it should be quite simple.

EMPEROR: Give a mech to a barbarian?

AIDEEN: Also, I can summon lightning to burn down your paper town. I should have mentioned that before.

EMPEROR: But mechs have always been exclusively Japanese!

BRIAN: Hippopotamus,
   As the leaves fall to the ground
   Mechs now leave Japan.

KEVIN: I'm not warning you again!

EMPEROR: I don't quite understand the bit about the hippopotamus.

AIDEEN: Are you summoning a mech?

EMPEROR: I've already summoned them. And they're coming up behind you!

AIDEEN: If you think I'm falling for that one—

KEVIN: No, they're there all right.

BRIAN: I think that's thirty warriors each, not counting the mechs. And the warriors have two very sharp swords each.

AIDEEN: Look, it's very simple. I just want one mech. Give it to me, or I cut your throat.

EMPEROR: Kill me, and die. My son will ascend the Chrysanthemum throne, and my honour will go with me to the grave unsmirched.

KEVIN: This isn't working.

AIDEEN: All right, will you sell me a mech? It's for the defence of my home against a terrible enemy. I can offer you a magic stick that can turn you into an eagle.

EMPEROR: Never!

BRIAN: Maybe we should leave and come back when we've got the gun.

EMPEROR: There are no guns allowed in Japan, by law.

KEVIN: How do you enforce that law?

EMPEROR: Mechs.

AIDEEN: So you'd really rather die than give us a mech?

EMPEROR: Much rather.

AIDEEN: All right then, thirty each it is, brothers.

BRIAN: I don't know what Father's going to say about this.

ACT IV

Scene 1: At sea, in the chariot

KEVIN: Brian, it's just a little cut, that's all. Don't be such a baby.

BRIAN: You're never fair to me. We should have held onto those apples.

AIDEEN: The Kingdom of the Cats is definitely not on this map.

BRIAN: I don't think going back into Kyoto with a fish would be a good idea at this point.

KEVIN: We'd never find that cat in the ashes anyway.

AIDEEN: I hope she got away.

BRIAN: Probably. Cats are quick.

AIDEEN: We don't want to go halfway around the world only to come back, if the Kingdom of the Cats happens to be near Japan.

KEVIN: Why would it be?

BRIAN: Why wouldn't it be?

AIDEEN: Let's go to Egypt. They worship cats there. That should be a good place to start.

KEVIN: Are you going to tell the king of the cats you're a poet come to visit his court?

AIDEEN: No, I think that trick's worn out. I think we'll either have to fight for it or persuade them to sell it to us.

KEVIN: Sell it? What do cats want? Fish?

BRIAN: Catnip?

AIDEEN: Respect?

QUEEN OF THE CATS: I couldn't help overhearing your conversation.

KEVIN: What? Where did you come from?

QUEEN OF THE CATS: What's the one thing you think you know about the king of the cats?

KEVIN: He has a black cloak of invisib—oh.

QUEEN OF THE CATS: I am the queen of the cats, and I've been watching you for some time. You'll be glad to know the cat in Kyoto did escape the fire and general destruction.

AIDEEN: I am glad. If you've been watching us, then you know what we want.

QUEEN OF THE CATS: You want my cloak, and you're prepared to go to any lengths at all to get it. You'd kill me, you'd kill every cat in the world if you had to.

KEVIN: It's true.

BRIAN: But I don't know what Father would say!

QUEEN OF THE CATS: You told the emperor that you needed the mech to defend your homeland, but the truth is that you need it to pay a fine for murder.

AIDEEN: It's true. Both are true. We need it to pay the fine, but Lugh needs it to defend Ireland against Cromwell.

229

QUEEN OF THE CATS: Who's Cromwell?

BRIAN: He's the king of the English.

KEVIN: He's not. He's not their king. He killed their king, and he refuses to replace him. He's the lord protector. And he's terrible. He's covered in terrible warts, and he's always sure he's right, and he praises God and passes the ammunition. The last time he came to Ireland he won such a great victory against us that we've only just recovered from it. He's coming back because our new king is his grandson, and there's a prophecy that his grandson will kill him.

QUEEN OF THE CATS: Why is his grandson your king?

AIDEEN: We elected him. He's eligible, he's one of the royal kin.

QUEEN OF THE CATS: I still don't understand. Why does he want to kill his own grandfather?

AIDEEN: Cromwell knew about the prophecy so he locked his daughter up in a tower and didn't let her marry.

QUEEN OF THE CATS: That trick never works.

AIDEEN: Kian, who was in England learning about guns, climbed in through a tower window, and the result was Lugh. Cromwell was off fighting battles, and when he came back Lugh had grown up in the tower—he climbed down and came to Ireland, just one step ahead of his grandfather's army, the famous Ironsides. Then we made him king after he proved that he was better than everyone else at everything important. So you can see he hates his grandfather, and his grandfather's men.

QUEEN OF THE CATS: Do you think Lugh would let me have my cloak back after Cromwell was defeated?

BRIAN: Oh yes, sure to.

AIDEEN: I think you'd have to ask him. You're welcome to come with us. We just have one more stop, if we can count on the cloak.

QUEEN OF THE CATS: Where's that?

KEVIN: Rome.

QUEEN OF THE CATS: Ah, Rome. Rome is a great cat city, I know it well. We stalk among the ruins of the empire. Kittens play among fallen pillars, and we drink water from ancient aqueducts.

BRIAN: You're coming with us?

QUEEN OF THE CATS: I wouldn't miss it.

Scene 2: Rome

AIDEEN: They've closed the gates, they must be expecting a siege. Ho, Gatekeeper?

POPE: Who's there?

AIDEEN: Is that you up on top of the wall, Holy Father?

POPE: Yes it is. I'm the pope of Rome. Who are you?

AIDEEN: It's Aideen, and Kevin, and Brian, with the queen of the cats.

POPE: The children of Tureen?

AIDEEN: Yes, the children of Tureen, from Ireland.

POPE: Go away.

KEVIN: He doesn't seem very pleased to see us.

POPE: I heard what you did to Machu Picchu, and to Kyoto, and I don't want you doing it here!

AIDEEN: Are you all alone up there?

POPE: No! But even if I was all alone up here, if all my Swiss Guards and cardinals had run away at the rumour that you were coming, I'd still have my alchemic gun, that can kill a thousand armoured fighters with one shot. And there are only three of you.

QUEEN OF THE CATS: Four, but who's counting?

AIDEEN: Holy Father, if you give us the gun, we'll go away and never bother you again. Furthermore, we'll use it to fight against Cromwell, and he's your enemy too.

POPE: But what shall I do if the antipope comes?

BRIAN: You're armoured in the Holy Spirit.

POPE: Oh all right then, come up and take it, just so long as you go away and leave me in peace.

KEVIN: Did the Swiss Guards really run away just at the news that we were coming?

BRIAN: We're heroes. They knew they couldn't stand against us.

KEVIN: I'd have thought better of them.

QUEEN OF THE CATS: I can't think why. From the evidence of their knives, they spend most of their time drinking wine, filing their nails, and picking their teeth.

Scene 3: Lugh's Hall. Present are LUGH and DANU, TUREEN, AIDEEN, BRIAN, KEVIN, and the QUEEN OF THE CATS.

AIDEEN: We have the chariot, gun, the cup, the clockwork toy, and the feather. We brought you the apples already.

LUGH: Good, good. So it's just the three shouts on a hill left, is it?

TUREEN: You forgot the black cloak.

KEVIN: This is the queen of the cats. She's come here with us. She has the cloak, but she wants to talk to you before giving it to us.

LUGH: Go on then, what do you have to say for yourself?

QUEEN OF THE CATS: If I give the children of Tureen my cloak of darkness, and they give it to you, I'd like you to promise to give it back to me after Cromwell is defeated.

LUGH: What? Why?

QUEEN OF THE CATS: It is my people's protection, to be able to move unseen in the darkness, a shadow in shadow. I am willing to lend that to you, but not to give it up forever.

LUGH: Then the fine is not paid, and even after his children have given their three shouts there will be a feud between me and Tureen for the death of my father.

TUREEN: If it has to be, it has to be.

DANU: Be reasonable, Lugh. They've brought you everything else. And you'd have the use of the cloak when you need it.

QUEEN OF THE CATS: This is not to do with Tureen and his

children. This is between you and me, King Lugh, between you and the cats.

DANU: Be kind, dearest.

LUGH: I don't see why I should be kind. What have the cats ever done for me, that I should consider them? The children of Tureen killed my father, and they promised to make restitution. Did I say the loan of a black cloak? No, I said a black cloak, and they all swore.

QUEEN OF THE CATS: You would strip my people of their protection, I can strip you of yours.

DANU: Have pity on the cats, Lugh, say you will give back the cloak.

LUGH: I need the cloak, and I deserve the cloak, and they said they would give me the cloak, and I see no need to make any new bargains concerning the cloak.

QUEEN OF THE CATS: What year is this?

DANU: Oh don't tell them!

AIDEEN: Tell us what?

QUEEN OF THE CATS: Your lord leaves me no choice.

BRIAN: It's the first year of the reign of King Lugh.

QUEEN OF THE CATS: And what year is it in the rest of the world?

KEVIN *[bravely]*: It's the year a new emperor ascends the Chrysanthemum Throne.

QUEEN OF THE CATS: The pope has an alchemical gun, the Japanese have mechs, the Incas are hiding in Machu Picchu, what time is this? What age?

LUGH: It is the age of heroes.

QUEEN OF THE CATS: The age of heroes, the age of myth, the day everything happens all muddled together, the day mechs can walk and heroes can kill thirty men each and burn down a city, and Irish is spoken everywhere in the world.

KEVIN: It's a good time.

QUEEN OF THE CATS: A good time if you're a hero, a time that never was.

LUGH: Madam, stop now. I will give back your cloak as soon as I have defeated Cromwell.

QUEEN OF THE CATS: It's too late. You can never defeat Cromwell. If you lived at all you lived and died before he was ever born.

LUGH: He is my grandfather.

QUEEN OF THE CATS: How paradoxical!

BRIAN: I don't understand.

QUEEN OF THE CATS: You are all legends, you're half-remembered stories, mixed together, changed on the tongue. You can do nothing, affect nothing, change nothing. You come from different times and different myths, drawn together now by nothing more than the force of story.

TUREEN: I can see through the walls.

DANU: I could always see through the walls. Now I can see through the floor.

QUEEN OF THE CATS: You're nothing but a—

AIDEEN: I could change you into a pig.

QUEEN OF THE CATS: And what will that achieve? You know now that you are no more than fragments. You can't forget that. You're not real, your battles are not real, the world you live in is made of fragments and tatters. None of it matters. I am a cat, and were I a pig it would be the same, I would be real under the sunlight and you would be only dreams, insignificant, turning to dust and smoke when examined closely.

DANU: You make us shabby and unsubstantial, but we were glorious.

LUGH: We were glorious, once.

KEVIN: We have to give three shouts on a hill.

QUEEN OF THE CATS: And what will you shout? That you are myths, unravelling on the wind?

AIDEEN: Three shouts, on a hill. That's real. That's necessary.

LUGH: Three shouts on a hill. The force of story requires it. And you may keep your cloak, I don't need even to borrow it.

DANU: You are in this story too, Queen of the Cats. Cats may be real under the sunlight, but are they sarcastic? Can they even talk?

QUEEN OF THE CATS: Call it a story. It's barely more than a pantomime, patched together out of scraps, cultural appropriation on a grand scale, an old story of collecting plot-tokens suddenly set on a whole planet. If you're not heroes, you're nothing, and you're not—

BRIAN: We are heroes, and we have to give three shouts on a hill.

QUEEN OF THE CATS: And where is your hill?

Act V

Glastonbury Tor

DANU: It's Glastonbury Tor. Look, here we are, standing on its bare green top. Ireland lies off to the west, and all around us are the green hills and dales of England.

AIDEEN: Buried under our feet lies King Arthur, the greatest legend of them all, sleeping until his country needs him.

LUGH: I remember Arthur. He had a dog called horse.

QUEEN OF THE CATS: No cat though. We walk through your stories with our tails high.

TUREEN: This is the hill. This is the time and the place.

KEVIN: THE CHILDREN OF TUREEN HAVE COME TO GLASTONBURY.

QUEEN OF THE CATS: That's your first shout. The cloud-capped towers . . .

CROMWELL: Who dares disturb this mound where we have sworn perpetual silence?

TUREEN: Tureen of Ireland, his children, King Lugh, and Queen Danu, with the queen of the cats. We got tired of waiting for you to come back to Ireland to fight us, and came here to fight you.

CROMWELL: I beat you once, and I'll beat you again. Ironsides, advance!

LUGH: Tureen, take the cup. Prepare the mech, Brian. Get the gun ready, Kevin. Aideen, stand ready with the feather.

QUEEN OF THE CATS: Cromwell was dead himself generations before they had mechs.

CROMWELL: Consider in the bowels of Christ that ye may be mistaken, Cat.

TUREEN: It will be a good fight.

LUGH: We'll stand side by side one last time.

CROMWELL: Is that you, grandson? Back to plague me?

LUGH: It's prophesied that I'll kill you.

QUEEN OF THE CATS: Cromwell died in his bed on the night of a great storm. Isaac Newton, as a schoolboy, measured the force of that storm. Ow! Stop pelting me with apples!

CROMWELL: Old in my bed? What kind of death is that for a hero? We will defend our island—

QUEEN OF THE CATS: Whatever the cost may be?

CROMWELL: FORWARD, IRONSIDES!

KING ARTHUR: Who shouts on this mound and wakes me from my sleep? Does my country need me? Is the hour at hand?

CROMWELL: No, everything's under control, go back to sleep. I can defend England, I have no need of you.

ARTHUR: That's what I thought when I dug up the head of Bran. Are you the king of England?

CROMWELL: England is mine.

LUGH: But he is not the king, he refuses kingship. He melted down the crown and minted it for money.

ARTHUR: Then you are no friend of mine. Who are these others?

LUGH: I am Lugh of the Cunning Hand, king of Ireland.

ARTHUR: I think I've heard of you.

LUGH: This is my wife, Danu.

ARTHUR [trying to remember]: The Children of Danu?

LUGH [uneasily]: We have no children.

TUREEN: I am Tureen, and this is my daughter, Aideen, and my sons, Kevin and Brian.

ARTHUR: Oh, you have the Holy Grail! I'm so glad it's been found. What year is this?

QUEEN OF THE CATS: You're not real either. You probably never existed.

CROMWELL: Who gave so much power to a talking animal?

KEVIN: Are we going to fight or not?

ARTHUR: It seems to me that the question is, who is going to fight whom?

TUREEN: It seems to me that the question is, why are we fighting?

DANU: Or to put that another way, what are we fighting for?

QUEEN OF THE CATS: You're fighting to exist.

KEVIN: We're fighting for heroes to exist.

AIDEEN: And magic.

QUEEN OF THE CATS: You're fighting for the world of fantasy?

ARTHUR: That seems like a good cause.

CROMWELL: But what a world it is! Ungodly, lacking in religious feeling, decadent, implausible, full of kings and gimmicks— it's hardly worth fighting for.

KEVIN: Full of heroes and honour.

AIDEEN: Full of dragons and poets.

KEVIN: Full of magic and promise.

BRIAN: Full of horses and stewpots.

QUEEN OF THE CATS: But what a patchwork world, full of half-understood feudalism, kings and conquests and magic items you quest for and don't even use.

CROMWELL: Talking animals . . . and kings are petty tyrants. Why do you imagine the world full of kings?

ARTHUR: Kings don't have to be tyrants.

AIDEEN: There was no king of the Americans.

DANU: It is what we know, written large, remembered, reflected on a bigger screen. It's what we care to remember. The world of heroes is a world where honour matters. They could have stayed in those far countries. Nobody doubted that they would come back to give three shouts on a hill. It's a world where good and evil are clear and defined.

BRIAN: Except that we did murder Kian, though I hate to mention it.

ARTHUR: Exactly what happened?

BRIAN: We were walking along, and this old man came walking the other way. He demanded that we get out of the way, in the rudest possible way. He drew his sword. So Aideen turned him into a pig.

AIDEEN: It would have worn off in an hour.

BRIAN: But he didn't wait, he came running up to us and knocked Kevin off his feet. Kevin drew his sword, and the pig ran at me and knocked me down in the mud. He was running at Aideen, and Kevin—

KEVIN: I insisted that she turn him back into a man, so that we could kill him, because it was beneath our dignity to kill a pig. She turned him back, and he went straight for her, sword out— and we killed him.

LUGH: I wouldn't have believed you could make me laugh telling the story of the death of my father.

TUREEN: When we talk about kings and queens, often it's a way of talking about a family.

QUEEN OF THE CATS: You're none of you real.

AIDEEN: Magic is real.

BRIAN: Honour is real.

ARTHUR: Somebody must rule.

QUEEN OF THE CATS: You can't go on existing now you know you're not real and your world isn't real.

KEVIN: I have an alchemical gun here, it was mentioned in Act I and it hasn't been fired. I could use it to break the fourth wall.

TUREEN: Where would we be then, Fourth Street?

BRIAN: We don't need to break it. We haven't given our third shout.

DANU: What should we shout?

KEVIN: We exist?

TUREEN: But once we shouted, we wouldn't exist any more. It's only the force of story that's keeping us here now we know what we are.

AIDEEN: Fantasy matters?

ARTHUR: It's not a creed to shout from the rooftops. It either matters or it doesn't.

QUEEN OF THE CATS: Rosencrantz and Guildenstern are—

CROMWELL: Talking animals are anathema.

DANU: Come on everybody, let's all give it together.

ALL: THREE SHOUTS ON A HILL!

POETRY

Dragon's Song

A wilderness of wings, bright glints of fire,
Dry wood burns fast, and long desire,
Coiled into curlicues, coins, a cup,
A thief in the night that drew me up.

What would I sing when the harp goes round?
An old wyrm's tale of underground?
Or a song of rising in spiralled flight,
Wide wings that flash with reflected light?

Or the human heroes who came so bold,
To challenge us and to steal our gold,
Who bade us fight them beneath the sun?
You know the names of the few who won.

I could sing of our wait till the final days

Till the root take flame in triumphant blaze
And the world-tree fall and the rainbow bend
And gods kill giants, and all things end.

My claws on the harp draw out each chord
Darkness, waiting coiled, the hoard,
A wilderness of wings, bright glints of fire
Dry wood burns fast, and long desire.

—*October 9, 2014*

Not in This Town

Did anyone wonder why he came this far,
To this town with one exit, one stop light, one bar,
Four neon churches, one high school, one park
Full of unspoken things taking place in the dark?

He drove in from the east in a big beat-up car.
Long shaggy dark hair, smiling eyes, a guitar,
Some hooch. All the girls of the town just went wild,
Not knowing at first he was Semila's child.

"Oh no, not in this town, unmarried," they said,
Her dad cast her out, said for him she was dead,
Her sister pretended she didn't exist
With her belly that proved she did more than get kissed.

Must be twenty years now since she went to the bad,
Since she cursed them and left, since she swore she was glad

To get out of this town, narrow, biased, and dumb,
Stalking off to the exit she stuck out her thumb.

Not shamefaced, Semila, she stood there with pride
With her belly thrust out, with a baby inside
A truck slowed, two drivers, she hopped in-between
And that was the last time Semila was seen.

Her boy from the east went by "Leo." His car
Had rust-stains like ivy. He drove to the bar
And ordered a pitcher, then sat in the sun
Just strumming, as girls wandered up one by one.

Now Theo, his cousin, was quiet, uptight,
A young cop, with need to do everything right,
Never drunk in his life, never stepped on a crack,
A good boy he was, who cut nobody slack.

Their mothers were sisters, Semila and Gail,
One passionate proud, and one fluttering frail.
Their boys were like betta-fish, spoiling to fight
When they clashed in the bar there on Leo's first night.

"Hey stranger, hey foreigner, get out of town,"
Theo said. Leo raised up a brow, sitting down,
While his cousin was standing in threatening pose
And Leo smiled lazily: "Do you suppose,

You might drink with me?" Leo asked, "Cousin of mine?
Drinking and dancing is nearly divine,
Let go, dance a little, and drink from my cup

And I'll leave you in peace here to let you grow up."

"I'm too young to drink beer. And I don't know your face?"
"I'm the son of Semila. You'd say her disgrace?"
"Did you card him?" called Theo. "He's not twenty-one!"
And he took a step back, with his hand on his gun.

Leo spread out his hands with placatory smile
And walked out of the bar, and the girls all the while
Were cooing and flirting and whispering "Oh!"
While Theo gave warnings they watched Leo go.

He camped in a barn on the edge of the park
Distant hum of the highway, a dog's lonely bark
And the sound of his music that wove through the dusk
Like sandalwood, ambergris, jasmine, and musk.

Strong perfume hung over the town the next day
A whiff of exotic that called folk to play,
Alluring and tempting, the sound of his notes,
Drifting in on the wind, like a warmth in their throats.

Not a woman in town could resist him, most men
Went out once or twice, drank with Leo, and then
He'd let them alone, only Theo refrained,
But the girls day and night danced his dance unrestrained.

Singing and dancing and drinking all hours
And chasing all over with kissing and flowers
Free love and free music, and hooch up for sale,
"No, not in this town!" Theo threw him in jail.

Leo stood at the window and sang through the bars
Wove the world in his song, from the hum of the cars
And light-tripping feet, from his mother's old shame
When the town cast her out and attributed blame.

Through the long afternoon, as the memory of scorn
Built the whisper of wind through the ripening corn
Dust devils rose spiralling, dancing along,
And the weight of the sun built the power of his song.

Every female in town then, from puberty on,
Ran off to the park, every woman was gone
Teenagers to grannies, run wild on the hill
And they couldn't be caught and they wouldn't stay still.

The high school half-empty, the churches bereft
Whole town half-deserted, no woman was left,
And no one could stop them, and no one would dare,
Till Theo found out his own mother was there.

His mother was gone, so he marched to the jail:
"Make them stop, I demand it! My poor mother, Gail!"
And Leo smiled slyly and said, "Would you see
What wild women look like, when once they get free?

This town tossed out my mother without half a thought.
You wouldn't drink with me, afraid to get caught,
Daren't dance the wild dances, intoxicate, oh
No never in this town, I know you won't go."

"Don't call me a coward," said Theo. "My mother
Needs rescuing now—be a cousin, a brother."
"You need my help now? Well such aid has a cost."
"I'll pay it," said Theo, and thus he was lost.

"It's hard to get near them, so dress as a girl.
Let me make up your face, prink your hair with a curl.
They won't suspect, cousin, drink this and advance,
And you're sure to catch sight of the girls in their dance."

"I must find my mother." "But what about mine?"
"Your mother, Semila? Is she here? That's fine."
"Take my keys, you should drive, coz," is all Leo said.
Theo drove along Main Street, blazed straight through the red.

Then the drink in his veins and the madness took hold,
Filled with fear for his mom, and the things he'd been told,
And Leo directing: "Turn left here. Now stop.
Get out of the car. Dance, don't look like a cop."

Theo danced as he went, and they tore him apart,
His own mother's fingernails ripped out his heart
And she woke to discover her deed, poor sad Gail.
In the end it's a punishment quite out of scale.

Don't bring on disaster refusing to bend
When people screw up try to act like a friend
Let humans be human and choose their own fate,
Accept the small madness to ward off the great.

—*March 13, 2016*

JO WALTON

Hades and Persephone

You bring the light clasped round you, and although
I knew you'd bring it, knew it as I waited,
Knew as you'd come that you'd come cloaked in light
I had forgotten what light meant, and so
This longed for moment, so anticipated,
I stand still, dazzled by my own delight.

I see you, and you see me, and we smile
And your smile says you are as pleased as me
With everything and nothing still to say
All that we've saved and thought through all this time
Boils down to affirmation now as we
Stand here enlightened in my realm of grey.

Cerberus wags his solitary tail,
And though the dust of Hell lies round our feet
Your flowers are already sprouting through.
"You came," "I said I would," "You didn't fail,"
"And you're still here," "Of course. We said we'd meet."
"Yes," "Yes!" "You're really here! "And so are you!"

We don't say yet that you will have to go
And Hell return inevitably black
Your flowers fade when parted from your tread
Though this is something we both surely know,
As certain as you come, you must go back,
And I remain alone among the dead.

They say I snatched you from the world above

252

Bound you with pomegranates, cast a spell
Bribed you with architecture. It's not so.
Friendship is complicated, life is, love,
Your work the growing world, my task is Hell
You come back always, always have to go.

But here and now, this moment, we can smile,
Speak and be heard, this moment we can share
And laugh, and help each other to be great,
And talk aloud together, all worthwhile,
Our work, our worlds, and all we really care,
Each word shines golden, each thought worth the wait.

And Hell's poor souls whirl round us as they glide
Off up to Lethe to begin again,
On to new lives, new dawns beyond Hell's night.
We walk among your flowers, side by side,
Such joys we share are worth a little pain.
You come back. And you always bring the light.

—April 2014

The Death of Petrarch

He fell asleep, reading in Cicero
And as he turned the page, in his last sleep
He found it didn't end, so he could keep
On reading the *De Gloria*, and know.

Forgetting meals, forgetting pain and age,

One book led to another, all made new,
Laid out before him, beautiful and true.
In such delight he'd greet each fresh-turned page.

And there lies Homer, that most glorious peak,
Poliziano's Homer, and it said
This was a Florentine who knew his Greek,

The Pope was back in Rome, and he was dead,
The world renewed, and given tongue to speak.
Sing, Goddess, Petrarch's joy in what he read.

—*November 8, 2015*

Advice to Loki

Some other cultures' thoughts about revenge:
Some say it is a dish best eaten cold, but not
An option for your nature, is it? Plan and plot
But always you are leaping wildfire hot.

Marcus Aurelius said the best revenge
Is to be unlike Odin—excuse me, be unlike
The one who dealt the injury, in this case, Odin.
That doesn't help. (And he was first to strike.)

Others say when you plan revenge to dig two graves.
You did that. He is bound as much as you.
But maybe there were smoother ways to go,
You bound your own pain ever open too.

For oaths will only bind the honour-bound
Which Odin never was, not that I heard
He goes for his advantage every time.
You at least kept the letter of your word.

All right, you did kill Baldur, his best son.
But who'd have thought he'd go this far for it?
He'd got your children too, all three of them.
. . . But did this really help the slightest bit?

You can't make people want you, you can make
Them do things, sometimes, but desire
Of any kind, for anything, is inside them,
And not compellable by ice or fire.

I'm sorry. I have also snarled on this
Too often, and with less excuse than you,
And lies and cunning mostly make it worse,
We have to face it that it's really true.

Some people say revenge is living well—
I've found it sometimes works to go away
And *be more awesome*. Let him sit alone,
To watch your wildfires leaping as you play.

Of course, you're still alone, and you still care.
But honestly, in time may come new gods.
(I found one, though I never thought I would
A better one than him.) There are some odds.

And even grimly going on and on
Can work, because of petty joys that life
(I'm not a Viking) showers freely down,
Creating, conversation, trees, fresh strife.

You think you're equals, but that isn't so.
You're *better* than he is. Like yourself more.
You're worth it, and he's such a selfish prick.
Go do new things, burn brighter than before.

It hurts to think of you a ball of hate
Waiting to burn the whole world down to black
Just because Odin sucks. Let go and weep,
Heal Yggdrasil, get free, then don't look back.

—*May 2013*

Ask to Embla

When we stood mute, rooted,
We grew side by side
Shared storms and seasons,
Drank from deep waters,
Flowered and fruited,
Washed by the same tides
Swayed for the same winds
knowing no reasons.

Three gods came out of the dark
Warming and changing and moving and shaping

Filling us up with their spark
I can step from this shore
This edge where we belonged before
To turn and see and speak and know
As root and branch knew how to grow.

As flesh transforms from wood,
I turn to you to start to speak
Believing I'll be understood:
"This world is a wonder,
The gods are a wonder,
And you . . ."

The words, the worlds, and we
New made in new sun's icy dawn
The slate-flecked sea, the very stones
Transmuted out of Ymir's bones,
The landscape, like us, all newborn
As we were turned from tree . . .

The same, and not the same, and you
Are gloriously different too
Now I can move and see and learn,
My life-spark blazes and I burn
To speak that you can answer me,
To say: "The world, the wonders, gods,
Our transformation," urgently,
"And you . . ."

And time and change and hope and all
The stories that have yet to be,

Together, reaching out, to build
All that a man who was a tree
Can dream, a name, a home, a hall,
A saga, and you in them all,
You, who are like the gods,
Like me, a wonder, and free-willed.
(And standing staring back at me
Though all the world stands bare to see.)

I draw my new-won breath to speak:
"The world's full of wonders,
The future's a wonder
The gods are a wonder
And you . . ."

—*May 2013*

Three Bears Norse

An old home, a bear home, remote from human-haunts,
Wall-girt and weather-warded, where ones wise in woodcraft
Lick into new life, a baby, a bear cub,
Safe among saplings, far in the forest.

Till one comes slyly, girlchild, goldilocks,
Soft-handed, secret-seeker, pamperling, pretty one,
"No!" never heard she, dancing like dandelion,
Stealing twixt tree-boughs, spies out the bear-house.

Fast closed stands the door, all bears gone from home,

In rushes Dandelion, door-breaker, greedy one,
No thought spares she for holy guest-law,
Spoiled child, undenied, heart set on plunder.

First seizes three chairs, orderly, big to small,
Claims each and tries each, breaking the smallest.
Next finds the oat-slop, orderly, big to small,
Claims each and tries each, eating the smallest.

Onwards goes Dandelion, breaker of guest-law,
Turning from oat-slop, yawning, bedwards,
Slinks up the stairs, three beds, big to small,
Orderly, tries each, sleeps on the smallest.

Bears, heading homewards, sleepy as sun seeks sea,
Father foremost, bear-cub beside him, bear-mother guarding rear,
Stop still, scent surprise, coming on cautiously
See their door open stands, blowing on wild winds.

"Who?" asks bear-father, "Dared to sit in my chair?"
"Who?" growls bear-mother, "Dared to sit in my chair?"
"Who," howls bear-cub, "Dared to sit in my chair,
Breaking it to scattered shards? I vow revenge."

"Who?" asks bear-father, "Dared to taste my oat-slop?"
"Who?" growls bear-mother, "Dared to taste my oat slop?"
"Who," howls bear-cub, "Dared to eat my oat-slop,
Eating it all up? I vow revenge!"

Upstairs, at long last, learn of the lawbreaker,
Sleeping serenely, stuffed with their oat-slop,

Wakes for an instant, seeing them, simpers, screams,
Bear teeth, bear claws, shred her, sunder her,
so perish lawbreakers.

—*August 29, 2006*

Machiavelli and Prospero

"Piero Soderini to Niccoli Machiavelli, 13 April 1521

My very dear Niccolo. Because the affair at Ragusa was not satisfactory to you, since Lord Prospero has asked me to recommend
a man capable of managing his affairs and I know your trust-
worthiness and your ability, I proposed you to him . . ."

> —From: *Machiavelli and His Friends: Their Personal
> Correspondence*, translated and edited by
> James B. Atkinson and David Sices, page 334

The Swiss. The French. His Holiness. The King of Spain.
And now this bookish Duke back to Milan
Just where he was before? Antonio was twice the man.
He followed his advantage, his own gain.

And Soderini thinks I'd work for him? That I'd enfold
My fortunes with that duke tossed in a boat
a scarecrow, broken staff and tattered coat,
And I to run his state, simply for gold?

What if it's true there's magic, that somehow

He summons spirits from the earth and sky?
And maybe he would teach those arts to me?

Well, nothing. Let him manage now
And I'll stay here and write, and ponder why,
And each of us stay in our library.

—*2013*

Cardenio

Cardenio's bones lie in an unmarked grave
beyond the bonny sallie willow grove
beside the shallow pool, none bend to grieve
no bannered tomb, only a hallowed groove.

Cardenio's dreams lie in a fallen snarl
of lost intentions, fallow, slow as snail
the filings of his plan, through those who kneel
or fill their glass with drams to toast his name.

Cardenio's play is lies and bones of dreams
procession of the willing, swelled with drums
with all the words unmarked, the swill, the drones
all hollow pomp of lost forgotten dramas.

For leaves will turn and fall as heads grow grey
Hell holds no harrow now, and dreams decay.

—*February 5, 2013*

Ten Years Ahead: Oracle Poem

Tomorrow's trends swirl in a pixel glow
Shaken and stirred and tipped in cups to go:
Drink deep, peer close, guess what we cannot know.

Ten years is long, and yet, not long enough,
Changes sift down unseen, or fast and rough,
In politics, in tech, in fights, in fluff.

Upon this planet shall be constant war,
Cod will come swarming back to Iceland's shore,
Today's new fads become a facile bore.

Nations will borrow all the banks will lend.
We will print perfect statues, and this trend
Will fill our houses with them, and then end.

With oracles reopening in Greece,
One war will end in unexpected peace,
Others go on and on with no surcease.

The unheard find a voice and have their say.
China and Spain declare free marriage day.
Democracy comes to the USA.

Fast and ubiquitous and very neat,
The word "computer" becomes obsolete.
As screens you cannot touch seem incomplete.

One thing you'd never guess will catch on here.

Mummies and Termites cause box office fear.
Cold fusion will be very very near.

Old age will keep receding as we age.
Books become beautiful on every page.
The net will bring us friendship, hope, and rage.

Doctors do miracles, but people die,
We'll get no closer to a reason why.
We send more robots up to search the sky.

But I'll still write in Protext '91,
And you'll get famous and have lots of fun,
And all the best of life be just begun.

Thus incrementally, as lives unfold,
We'll change unnoticing until we hold
Our different world the same, its tale untold.

Bad mixed with good, safe, scary, normal, strange,
Ten years of human choice and human range,
The only certainty in life is change.

—*May 2015*

Pax in Forma Columba

Come, peace, descend to us now
in the form
of an urban pigeon.

Underfoot everywhere, disregarded,
fed by children on sugar biscuits,
and by old people on hoarded crumbs.

Flocking all over, rising up at a sudden alarm
to settle back in a flutter of wings,
unafraid, beautiful, ubiquitous.

Grey, barred, or brown,
with a preen of glorious pink,
bright-eyed, head cocked, bold.

Descend into the interstices of our lives,
peck round our park benches, strut past our summits,
nest on our ledges, circle our rooftops.

Billing and cooing, pouting and searching,
come down to the hearts of our cities
and be everywhere taken for granted.

—*June 24, 2016*

Translated from the Original

When they came down to the
Water/shore/spaceport/edge
They embarked and took ship for
The lagoon/lacuna/Lagos/the ledge
The/a sun was occluded/eclipsed

264

Glinting
There was no doubt, none any more,
Hinting
. . .
In the archipelago/far settlement/sea-carved land,
Only their footprints, dissolving in sand.

—*December 15, 2014*

Sleepless in New Orleans

The moon has set
and the fucking Pleiades
and I have to be on a train at seven o'clock this morning
but here I am
writing poetry under the covers
as if I am twelve.

I have to tell you that last June
in the front row of a Fringe performance
of Euripides' *Hippolytos*
I accepted a blood red cherry from the manicured hand
of a drag queen Aphrodite.
I thought "Take, eat . . ."
and my soul said "You have always been good to me,
Foam-born Peleia
but seriously? Have you noticed I am menopausal
and suited as things are?
You *really* would surprise me."

Wouldn't you think I'd know better?

Clearly, this is her votive city
she must get tired of the pap she is offered
the same masks over and over.

We are from different shores
of the same planet
and speak the same language
and I am here.
I do not ask anything
but let's go to Venice
and Constantinople
and keep talking the stars into a new sky
where maybe words reach.

—*February 25, 2013*

The Godzilla Sonnets

i) Godzilla vs Shakespeare
Up on the ramparts all await their time
Each heroine, the fools and knaves, each king,
Ready to catch our hearts, the play's the thing
A cockpit where they arm themselves with rhyme.

The monster tries to hide, but shows through plain,
Behind a frond ripped up with giant claws
We see his scaly hide and gaping jaws
As Birnam tropics come to Dunsinane.

All rally to defend now, each with each,
Juliet with dagger, Richard on a horse,
Dear Hamlet with his poisoned foil of course,
Harry with swords and longbows, at the breach.

Godzilla, shuffling closer, knows what's what.
Size matters. But then so do prose and plot.

ii) Godzilla in Shakespeare
She was too big to sneak, she couldn't hide,
She did well at Harfleur, the wall went down,
If Bardolph then got splatted in the town
All well and good, Flewellyn got to ride.

Verona fell out differently, no feud
Of family could stand against those feet
She could go nowhere that required a street
Dancing or love-making, too big, too crude.

When troops were needed, she advanced before,
She sheltered Lear on the blasted heath
She stood outside, or waited underneath,
And lurked before the walls of Elsinore.

She couldn't seem sincere as Romeo.
As Caliban she really stole the show.

iii) Godzilla Weeps for Baldur
A little Viking boat, with tattered sail,
Frigg, by the curved carved prow, bids everyone

To weep for Baldur, her lost murdered son
To bring him back from Hel, she cannot fail.

She's what, a radioactive dinosaur?
Destruction manifest, and Japanese?
Frigg begged her, even deigning to say please
And left her sitting weeping by the shore.

Aesir and monsters close beneath the skin
Berserk rampager—Frigg could work with that
She told her what they'd lost, and as they sat
Godzilla wept for Baldur, as for kin.

So what was Baldur that Godzilla cared?
Each cherry-blossom petal that she'd spared.

iv) Godzilla in Love
It is the nightingale and monsters all
Come tripping through the glades of some strange wood
Godzilla sulking, trying to be good
All balconies inevitably fall.

(All right, she stomped Verona *really* flat.)
But this is different, this is fairy-time,
With transformations, turning on a dime
The size of others, and she longs for that.

Or failing that, some great iambic man,
Scaled up to her and talking like the Bard
They'd stomp together, would that be so hard?
Uncertain, frightened, questions if she can—

Does love change when it alteration find?
She wants someone to love her for her mind.

v) Godzilla at Colonos

Alive she is destruction, people flee
Mouths opened wide in screams before her tread
But that great body when it falls will be
A benediction after she is dead.

She raged and roared, but failed at family,
Her sons wreak devastation, fight and fall,
Her daughters seek to bury them, but see,
One destiny to perish over all.

But once there was an answer she could give
People and monster met in what they knew,
That time's inexorable, but people live,
And grow and change and die, and monsters too.

So though she threatened life and home and city
The faces hold not terror now, but pity.

—2015

Not a Bio for Wiscon

Jo Walton has run out of eggs and needs to go buy some,
she has no time to write a bio
as she wants to make spanakopita today.

269

She also wants to write a new chapter
and fix the last one.
Oh yes, she writes stuff,
when people leave her alone to get on with it
and don't demand bios
and proofreading and interviews
and dinner.
Despite constant interruptions
she has published nine novels
in the last forty-eight years
and started lots of others.
She won the Campbell for Best New Writer in 2002
when she was 38.
She has also written half a ton of poetry
which isn't surprising as she finds poetry
considerably easier to write
than short bios listing her accomplishments.
She is married, with one (grown up, awesome) son
who lives nearby with his girlfriend and two cats.
She also has lots of friends
who live all over the planet
who she doesn't see often enough.
She remains confused by punctuation,
"who" and "whom"
and "that" and "which."
She cannot sing and has trouble with arithmetic
also, despite living ten years in Montreal
her French still sucks.
Nevertheless her novel *Among Others*
won a Hugo and a Nebula
so she must be doing something right

at least way back when she wrote it
it'll probably never work again.
She also won a World Fantasy Award in 2004
for an odd book called *Tooth and Claw*
in which everyone is dragons.
She comes from South Wales
and identifies ethnically as a Romano-Briton
but she emigrated to Canada in 2002
because it seemed a better place
to stand to build the future.
She blogs about old books on *Tor.com*
and posts poetry, recipes, and wordcount on her LJ
and is trying to find something to bribe herself with
as a reward for writing a bio
that isn't chocolate.

Update, February 2016

Since then she has written another four novels
And the one she was interrupted writing a chapter of
My Real Children
won the Tiptree Award,
she also won the Locus Best Non-Fiction for her collection of
blog posts
and her son has broken up with his girlfriend.
She knows it's a cliché, but tonight's dinner will be stew,
followed by blackcurrant crumble,
because
she has run out of eggs.

ABOUT THE AUTHOR

Jo Walton has published thirteen novels, most recently *Necessity*. A fourteenth, *Lent*, is due out in 2018. She has also published three poetry collections and an essay collection. Walton won the John W. Campbell Award for Best New Writer in 2002; the World Fantasy Award for *Tooth and Claw* in 2004; the Hugo and Nebula awards for *Among Others* in 2012; and in 2014, the Tiptree Award for *My Real Children* and the Locus Award for *What Makes This Book So Great.*

Walton comes from Wales but lives in Montreal, where the food and books are much better. She plans to live to be ninety-nine and to write a book every year.